Code name: Thunder

"Do you believe in women's intuition?" she asked.

Max smiled slowly as the silence stretched between them. "What's your intuition tell you about me?"

Kris measured her words carefully. "You define yourself by the work you do and the secrets you keep. You've made a home for yourself among these secrets. But someday you may find they're not enough."

Max started to answer, then changed his mind. In his gut, he knew the truth when he heard it. But she was wrong about one thing. He'd accepted the need to keep the secrets he guarded—especially one. But there was no peace or sense of home inside him because of it. He was a man of facts with a secret that facts didn't support.

A stargazer.

He'd known what he wasn't supposed to know…information that could get them both killed if he made one miscalculated move.

AIMÉE THURLO

STARGAZER'S WOMAN

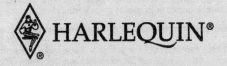

HARLEQUIN®

TORONTO • NEW YORK • LONDON
AMSTERDAM • PARIS • SYDNEY • HAMBURG
STOCKHOLM • ATHENS • TOKYO • MILAN • MADRID
PRAGUE • WARSAW • BUDAPEST • AUCKLAND

To Mitch, who knows where all the bodies are buried.
With special thanks to Lt. Col. Elizabeth S. Birch USMC
for her help.

ISBN-13: 978-0-373-69331-3
ISBN-10:   0-373-69331-1

STARGAZER'S WOMAN

ABOUT THE AUTHOR

Aimée Thurlo is a nationally known bestselling author. She's written more than forty novels and is published in at least twenty countries worldwide. She has been nominated for the Reviewer's Choice Award and the Career Achievement Award by *Romantic Times BOOKreviews* magazine.

She also cowrites the Ella Clah mainstream mystery series, which debuted with a starred review in *Publishers Weekly* and has been optioned by CBS.

Aimée was born in Havana, Cuba, and lives with her husband of thirty years in Corrales, New Mexico. Her husband, David, was raised on the Navajo Indian Reservation.

Books by Aimée Thurlo

HARLEQUIN INTRIGUE

*Four Winds
**The Brothers of Rock Ridge
†Sign of the Gray Wolf
††Brotherhood of Warriors

CAST OF CHARACTERS

Max Natoni—They said he was a stargazer, but he trusted his instincts as a former cop a lot more than the old medicine man's hocus pocus. As a warrior for the Brotherhood, his own training would be enough to protect his dead partner's sister.

Kris Reynolds—Her sister had been killed on assignment with Max Natoni while protecting a fortune in precious metal. Kris needed answers more than riches, but her heart kept getting in the way.

Hastiin Bigodii—The medicine man led by example, but Max followed his own rules.

John Harris—For a dead man, the former cop got around a lot. A killer who knew every trick in the book, even in death he couldn't be trusted.

Bruce Talbot—His job was to find a way to get the missing platinum back and save the reputation of his company. Was he just overzealous, or could he be the inside man in a crime gone awry?

Detective Lassiter—The retired marine had it out for Max, but he cut Kris a break—marine to marine.

Jerry Parson—When he and his crew weren't working over stolen cars, they were working over the competition—which included anyone who got in his face.

Deputy Robert Joe, aka Guardian—He was the Brotherhood of Warriors contact inside the sheriff's department, so why was he getting in the way?

Prologue

Max Natoni joined the circle of men gathered inside the cave of secrets. The red sandstone walls that surrounded them held the echoes of tradition and honor. It was that core of strength that had sustained the Brotherhood of Warriors under all circumstances.

The pungent scent of piñon from the small campfire in the center of the chamber filled the air, and the flames cast fleeting shadows on the faces of those gathered there. He could see loyalty and courage—their life's blood—indelibly etched on the features of each man present.

Max knew most of those gathered around the fire only by their code names—the only form of identification that would be used tonight. He'd be addressed as "Thunder," the name given to him by *Hastiin Bigodii,* the medicine man who currently served as their leader.

The Brotherhood of Warriors, established during the time of Kit Carson, was an impenetrable line of defense that stood between the tribe and its enemies. This elite force worked in the shadows—rarely seen but always felt. It existed so that the *Diné,* the Navajo people, could walk in beauty.

Much was demanded of anyone wanting to join their ranks. They'd undergo trials meant to break all but the strongest. Most ultimately failed. In the end, only the best of the best remained and earned the right to join the Brotherhood of Warriors.

Though he was staring at the fire, Max could feel *Hastiin Bigodii's* gaze on him.

"Thunder," *Hastiin Bigodii* said at last, "you're named for Yellow Thunder, who had the power to find things. You, too, have that gift, though you still haven't accepted it and learned how to use your ability."

Max started to argue, then clamped his mouth shut. He was a man who relied on facts. Logic was the only foundation he trusted. That's why he'd become a police officer, and later a detective, for an Anglo department outside the Rez.

Then the unimaginable had happened.

After that, Max had been forced to carve out a new life for himself. The land between the sacred mountains, the Rez, was his home now, and the men around him were his brothers in every way that counted. He wouldn't fail them.

"I *am* the man for this job," Max said. "John Harris, the ex-detective from the Farmington Police, betrayed us. Though my partner paid with her life, she also made sure Harris didn't find what he tried to steal—the tribe's platinum. I know the way my partner thinks—thought—and can figure out where she hid it." He released a deep breath. "She and I worked together as police officers for many years. That makes me the logical choice for this assignment. I ask the Brotherhood to give me a chance to complete what we started. Let me restore the harmony and balance, the *hózhg.*"

"Pride—and revenge—that's what's really driving you, isn't it?" The challenge came from a warrior known as Wind. Although Max and he were also first cousins, here, they were bound by something deeper than kinship—an unqualified allegiance to the Brotherhood of Warriors.

"It's more than that," Max replied firmly. "My partner died *defending* that platinum, but now her reputation's in question. Too many are convinced that she was involved in the theft, even though she forfeited her life protecting that shipment. Her sacrifice cries out for justice."

"You're too personally involved. That'll decrease your effectiveness. She was a well-paid courier who was hired to deliver the platinum our tribe purchased. That's all," another warrior he knew only as Smoke said, his voice a mere whisper. "She knew the risks."

Max looked at *Hastiin Bigodii*. In Navajo, the words simply meant "man with the bad knee." But his real name had power and would never be used lightly.

"I can fix this—I can right what went wrong," Max said in an even stronger voice.

"It's your gift—what brought you back here to us, Stargazer. That may, in the end, prove invaluable," *Hastiin Bigodii* said quietly, adjusting a piece of pine at the edge of the fire.

Max didn't answer. Gift? He had many words for it, but that had sure never been one of them.

"But you haven't developed your abilities, and without that…" *Hastiin Bigodii* added, leaving the sentence hanging.

"As you yourself have admitted on many occasions," Smoke pressed, "your abilities as a stargazer are questionable. Under the circumstances it's not much of an advantage. You're also saddled with personal baggage that could interfere with what you have to do. Someone with no ties to this case may be a better choice."

Smoke was lean and built for speed. Once during training, Max had seen him take down three of the Brotherhood's top fighters in a move so quick no one had even seen it coming. Max knew Smoke wanted the case, but this one was *his*.

"My connection to my partner's family will open doors that'll remain closed to anyone else," Max insisted. "I'll be seeing my partner's sister soon. She may not know me personally, but she's heard about me from her sister for years. That'll help foster trust between us. She's an asset I can use to help me do what needs to be done."

Silence settled over all the ones gathered there. At long last *Hastiin Bigodii* spoke. "Thunder, *you* are my choice. The insurance companies will take their time responding to the Tribal claim, and without the jewelry sales that platinum represents, our craftsmen will go hungry this winter. The tribe can't afford to wait." Though his voice dropped to a whisper, his words reverberated with conviction. "It's time for us to get to work. You'll have the full support of the Brotherhood behind you."

As the warriors left the chamber, Max hung back, knowing *Hastiin Bigodii* would have some final words for him.

Hastiin Bigodii remained seated next to the fire and across from Max. He didn't speak again until they were alone.

"Your *jish*," *Hastiin Bigodii* said, pointing Navajo-style with his lips to the medicine bundle at Max's waist. "Is the crystal there along with the other items I gave you?"

"Yes. I've also made sure the crystal is well coated in the pollen you gathered for me."

Hastiin Bigodii nodded in approval. "Keep the *jish* with you at all times and under all circumstances. During the time of the beginning, a crystal was placed in the mouths of our people so that their spoken words would come true. Pollen represents safety and well-being. Together, they become a prayer that'll draw those blessings to you."

"It's a powerful gift. Thank you," Max said with a nod.

Hastiin Bigodii said nothing for several long moments, then at long last spoke again. "Remember one thing. Your greatest strength is inside you. Honor who and what you are, and everything else will fall into place."

Max knew what he was referring to and felt obliged to point out a hard truth. "I've tried crystal gazing several times to find the answers we need, but nothing's come to me. Maybe I don't have the ability anymore...if I ever really did, that is."

"The missing child you found owes his life to your gift. What you did back then was *not* a product of logic and you know it," *Hastiin Bigodii* answered. "Let go—trust that there's more to life than what the eyes can see. In your heart you already know this."

Max didn't meet his gaze. To do so would have been seen as a sign of great disrespect. "The mind works better when the heart is kept out of the equation."

Hastiin Bigodii smiled, but said nothing as he stood and left.

Though Max had found the elder's reaction unsettling, he refused to dwell on it now. He had a job to finish.

Max smothered the burning embers with a bucket of sand left for that purpose, and departed the cave shortly thereafter. With the fading glow of the moon to show him the way, he climbed down the ladder to the piñon juniper forest below.

Clouds covered the blue-black sky and, as he reached the ground, thunder shook the earth beneath his feet. Max glanced at the growing storm clouds above him. Their anger mirrored his own. Sound and fury would be his soul's dark companions as he searched for answers in the days ahead.

Chapter One

Kris Reynolds adjusted her baseball cap, protecting her light brown eyes with the bill, and continued repotting a Great Basin Sage into a larger decorative pot.

She loved working with growing things—plants that would add character to any garden or household and give their new owners pleasure for years to come. It was part of the reason she'd opened Smiling Cactus Nursery, a place where she'd be sharing gardener's tips instead of survival tactics.

Though she'd served her hitch as a marine in a supposedly noncombat role, she'd seen more than her share of violence. She'd come home eager to find peace, and a healing of those wartime memories, but fate had stepped in and more tragedy had followed. Only a few days after her return, her only sister had been murdered. Death had been waiting by the roadside again just as it had been so often overseas. But there was one big difference. This time it was personal.

Thinking of Tina filled her with a familiar heaviness of spirit, and she swallowed quickly, hoping to stem the tears that usually followed. Tina had been her best friend, not just her sister. Kris could feel her absence every second of the day.

"You're thinking of Tina again, aren't you?" Maria Lucero observed, seeing Kris adjusting the gold four-leaf clover pendant that hung around her neck. On each leaf was a single letter—one side spelled Kris, the other, Tina.

Kris sighed. She missed Tina so much. Looking at her assistant, she nodded. "I can't believe she's really gone. What makes it even harder is that I still don't know *why* Tina died. The police won't tell me anything, except that she was on a courier run and on her way to the Rez from Arizona."

"You'll get the information out of them eventually," Maria said somberly. "It's not in your nature to give up."

Kris smiled. "It's the Marine in me. We never surrender."

"But, remember, you're not in the Corps anymore," Maria said softly.

Kris smiled. "Once you earn the title Marine, it's yours for life."

It was that discipline that would sustain her now. Before she was through, she'd know exactly why her sister had died. And if Tina had left unfinished business, she'd see it done as well. It would be her way of honoring her sister's memory.

Kris looked around her nursery for the umpteenth time. Her heart was home, and through this nursery she'd learn to welcome each new day again. But first there was one more duty to fulfill.

MAX PARKED IN FRONT of the Smiling Cactus Nursery and walked toward the open greenhouse door. As he stepped inside, he suddenly bumped into someone coming out, a woman wearing a baseball cap and shouldering a large plastic bag of potting soil.

As she fell back, the woman lost her grip on her bag and it came crashing down on top of his foot.

"Sorry," she said quickly, bending over to pick up the bag.

Unfortunately, he bent down at the same time and their heads collided with a resounding thud.

"My fault, sir, I'm so sorry! How about a ten-percent

discount on anything you buy today?" she added, checking the bag for holes.

Stepping back to avoid another bump and rubbing his forehead, he took a closer look at the woman's face. "It's you, isn't it? Kris Reynolds?"

As her gaze went up to his face, recognition flashed in her eyes. "Max Natoni? I went to see you at the hospital, but you were pretty much out of it at the time. How are you feeling?"

She was his former partner's spitting image—or nearly so. Yet where Tina's honey-brown eyes had been cold and hard—the long-term results of being a police officer—Kris's were lighter and softer somehow, like the scent of flowers that clung to her. All in all, not what he'd expected from a former marine.

"I'm doing much better, thanks," he said at last.

Max reached to pick up the bag, but she was faster. She grabbed it by the corners with perfectly manicured hands, and swung it into a nearby wheelbarrow before he could help. He'd always liked capable women, and Kris was obviously no exception. Her blend of toughness and femininity was an appealing contradiction.

"I've been hoping for a chance to talk to you," she said. "Why don't we go into my office?"

As she led the way, Max saw the huge smiling cactus on the back of her denim work shirt. Prickly but sweet? As his gaze drifted downward, he observed the way she filled out her jeans. The soft curve of her hips, and the way they swayed with each stride certainly held his attention. Definitely sweet—a few thorns never hurt anyone.

THE SECOND THEY ENTERED her small office, Kris stepped around her desk and reached for the bottle of aspirin she kept in her drawer. She offered him two, but he declined.

Kris made herself comfortable in her chair and regarded

Max Natoni thoughtfully as he took the seat by the window, shifting it around to face her directly. The dimples that flashed at the corners of his mouth whenever he smiled contrasted with the scar on his left cheek. There was something infinitely masculine about the man…and that killer smile…. It made her heart beat a little faster—something a battalion of jarheads had never quite managed to do.

Irritated with herself for getting soft, she glanced down at her desk. Heatstroke. That's why her heart was acting weird. Where was that water bottle? Since leaving the Middle East she'd stopped hydrating enough.

"I've been hoping for the chance to talk to you alone," Max said quietly, slipping his leather jacket off with a shrug and tossing it casually onto the corner coat rack's hook.

Kris knew that if she wanted to find out what had happened to her sister, Max was the key. "Tina respected you," she started, then saw him flinch. "Is that a surprise?" she asked.

He shook his head. "That's not it. Navajos don't speak the name of the dead out loud, particularly this soon after their passing."

Kris nodded. "I'm sorry. I'd forgotten about that. I meant no disrespect. I know how important it is to cling to your own culture—to the things that define you." She paused, organizing her thoughts. "My sister spoke highly of you—and often, too, I should add. That's why I'm hoping you'll help me now. I need to know what happened to her. Everyone I've spoken to so far, the sheriff's department, the Farmington police, the Tribal cops, give me the same answer. They're not free to talk about a case under investigation."

"What exactly have they told you so far about the way she died?"

"I know my sister was working with you and another man—another courier named Harris. Your objective was to protect some tribal assets. From the bits and pieces I overheard at the station, those assets were some kind of jewelry. Now I want the rest of the details."

"What led you to think jewelry was involved?" Max asked her.

"I overheard one of the detectives saying that the missing suitcase is worth over a half-million dollars. Then a few days later an investigator working for a company called Jewelry Outlet, a tall redhead by the name of Bruce Talbot, came by," she said. "The man was a pain in the butt. He hung around questioning my employees, and then tried to grill me. From his questions I know he believes that my sister—and I—had something to do with the robbery."

She met his gaze and saw how his dark brown eyes could change at a moment's notice. Yet it was his air of self-possession that intrigued her most.

"I won't allow that cloud of suspicion to remain over my sister or on me," she continued. "I have every intention of finding out *exactly* what went down. Then I'm going to prove that my sister's innocent, and that she died doing her job."

"Do you have any background in investigative work?"

"I have a logical mind and I was an intelligence analyst in the Corps. That'll be enough." She paused, then continued. "*Honor* is more than just a word to me. It's worth dying for."

"Your sister gave her life to protect tribal assets. Next time Talbot comes around, send him to me."

"I know you work for the tribe. But in what capacity? A courier? Security guard?" Judging from his neutral expression and his questions, he'd come with more than a social visit in mind.

He took out his card and handed it to her.

She studied it for a moment. "Security. Office of the Navajo Tribal President. That doesn't tell me much."

"I work on the President's behalf, carrying out whatever assignments come up," he answered, leaning back in his chair and stretching his long legs. "I'm an investigator who answers only to the tribe."

She held his gaze. The man was holding back. Instinct and training told her that, and much more. Keeping secrets was second nature to him. His body language attested to his ease with them.

While serving in the military, she'd had to do the same thing. She wondered if Max knew what a toll secrets eventually took on those who guarded them.

Almost as quickly as the thought had formed, she focused back on the situation at hand. "Those assets you won't identify—let's just call them jewelry for now. Talbot intimated that I might know where they are, so he's talking conspiracy."

"What did you tell him?"

"Not much. I, shall we say, *escorted* him off my property?" She watched his gaze skim over her lips, then drop lower, grazing her neck, and taking in the soft swell of her breasts. The look hadn't been insolent or disrespectful. It had been…appreciative.

Kris suppressed the shiver that touched her spine. He was playing her. He knew that nature had given him a certain amount of power over the opposite sex and he'd learned to use it. She wouldn't be taken in.

"Back to my sister…what happened?" she pressed again. "At one point, Talbot had the nerve to suggest that I'd previously met with Harris and that I knew where the stolen merchandise was." She paused. "He's lucky he can still walk upright."

"Harris is dead, but he was the key player. He betrayed the tribe, your sister and me," he said, then taking a breath continued. "We all set out in the same vehicle with our cargo, Harris driving. Our route took us through Four Corners, and you know how desolate that stretch is. Not long after we passed into New Mexico, he insisted on pulling over. He claimed that there was something wrong with the steering and he wanted to stop and take a look. We all got out and he suddenly pulled a gun on us. He shot me, then fired at your sister as she scrambled out of the backseat. I went down, but managed to return fire and force him back, giving your sister the chance to drive away with the cargo. Unfortunately, her only option was to head down a dirt road, not the highway."

She could picture it clearly. Tina would have done everything in her power to keep what had been entrusted to her out of a thief's hands. "What happened to you then?"

"I took a hit to the head, maybe from a second gunman, and passed out. I didn't wake up until the next day. Evidence at the scene suggests that Harris either had another vehicle hidden nearby, or was met shortly thereafter by a partner. We also have reason to believe Harris caught up to your sister *after* she hid the cargo."

"You found the car she drove off in," Kris commented thoughtfully. "Wasn't there any other evidence in or around it?"

"It had rained that afternoon, so the tracks in the area were almost indistinguishable by the time she was located. But I'm absolutely certain that your sister hid the assets we were protecting—and died with honor protecting them. Which brings me to the reason I'm here," he added. "My job now is to find out where she went, who she spoke to or saw, and where those assets ended up."

"So to you, this is mostly a matter of finding the missing cargo," she concluded. "But why do you need me for that? Why don't you just expand the search until you find the stuff?" She paused, suddenly reminded of Talbot. "Or did you come to me because you also think I had something to do with the theft?" Angry, she faced him squarely.

"No, that's not it." He rose to his feet and placed both his hands on her shoulders, capturing her gaze. "I'm here because I remember the way your sister spoke about you. She told me that you were two of a kind. I believe that if anyone can second-guess what she did that day, it'll be you."

Max was telling her the truth. She could feel it. But she was just as sure that there was a lot more he wasn't saying. "You two shared a working relationship," she said at last. "You were partners in the police force at one time, too. That should give you all the edge you need."

"Your sister and I respected each other, and we worked well as partners, but we were never anything more than that."

"My priority isn't finding those precious assets. I want to know exactly what happened to my sister that day and why she was killed. Since we have different goals, I can't see us working together."

"We'll have a better chance of finding answers—and staying alive—if we work together," he replied in quiet voice.

She gazed into his eyes, then shook her head and turned away. "I won't work with someone who's holding out on me. If you want us on the same team, then start by telling me what was stolen. I know how to keep things under wraps. If the United States Marine Corps trusted me, so can you."

"It's not that I don't trust you," he began.

"Then stop playing games," she interrupted sharply, bringing forth the bark that had served her so well as a marine. "If you want my help, then put me in the picture, and tell me everything you know. Otherwise, you're on your own."

"We're not overseas now, giving orders, or fighting a war. This type of case isn't part of your training. You're out of your element," he said, his eyes narrowed, his gaze sharp.

Kris was sure that not many people could have stood up to one of those icy looks of his, but she held her ground. "I'm a quick study. I intend to start by examining my sister's personal effects as soon as the police release them. I'll also have a talk with our senator and congresswoman and ask for their help in loosening some lips. I've got it covered, so it looks like we're through here," she added, gesturing to the door. "I've got a long day ahead of me."

"Give me a few more minutes of your time," Max said,

slipping his jacket back on and jamming his hands into the pockets. "My pickup is parked right out the side door. Walk with me, and we'll talk. You've got nothing to lose."

MAX WAITED FOR HER as she stepped over to speak to the woman at the cash register. Kris was one tough lady. Women usually liked him, but he'd tried charm and that hadn't worked. He'd also tried logic, but her points had been valid, too. He needed a new tactic—and fast.

A moment later she fell into step beside him. "Don't even *think* of trying to play me, Max. I've been dealing with men trying to tell me what to do for years."

The challenge sparked something inside him. She had fire, this one. He brought his thoughts under control quickly. Without control and finesse, he'd get nowhere.

"So talk," she said. "Time's wasting and I've got other work to do."

He was so completely focused on Kris that he didn't pay much attention to the van parked behind his pickup until the side door slid open. By then, it was too late.

Two men wearing topcoats and ski masks jumped out, the first one firing a taser directly at him.

The jolt stunned him instantly, like an electric sledgehammer. Then one of the contacts slipped out, having hit the button on his leather jacket instead of lodging in place. Shaking off the attack, he reacted, striking out with a jab even before turning to face his assailant.

Dropping the taser, the man advanced with his fists. Max's defense was quick. He blocked a jab, then delivered a hard uppercut to the surprised man's jaw.

Out of the corner of his eye, he caught a quick glimpse of Kris. As the other thug made a grab for her arm, she landed a spearlike kick to his left thigh, barely missing a crippling strike to the groin. The man sagged back.

Catching a glimpse of movement out of the corner of his

eye, Max glanced back at his own opponent, and saw him reach for a sawed-off shotgun inside his topcoat.

"Gun!" Max yelled, knowing he was too far away to grab the weapon in time.

Leaping to one side, he grabbed Kris by the arm and pulled her around the front bumper of a small SUV. They fell to the gravel just as the shotgun blast shattered the driver's side window.

Chapter Two

Max had rolled to the left, simultaneously reaching for the gun at his waist. Kris immediately reached down her right side for her service Beretta. Old habits died hard. All she found now were pruning shears in a leather holder at her belt.

Two more shotgun blasts shook the vehicle they were hugging. "We need them *alive*," one of the men called to the other.

Kris saw Max's reaction and wondered if he'd recognized the voice. But there was no time to discuss that now.

They waited, back to back, crouched low beside the passenger's side front tire. "Stay close to the tire so they can't see our feet. Let them come to us," she whispered, taking a quick look underneath the vehicle, trying to locate their assailants. "I can take down the one who came after me. He's an amateur."

Max turned toward the back end of the SUV. "I'm going to the rear axle and take a quick look. Maybe I can get a drop on the one with the shotgun."

"No, stick close and cover my back. You can't fire in that direction anyway. A stray bullet could kill a civilian. Make them come to us," she repeated.

He glanced back at her and realized that he was taking tactical advice from a woman wearing a shirt with a smiling cactus. Before he could give that further thought, she reached into her shirt pocket for her cell phone and dialed 9-1-1.

"Deputies are on their way," she called out a second later.

They heard running footsteps, followed by the distinctive slam of the van door being pulled shut.

As the van's engine started up with a roar and they heard the squeal of tires, Max stood.

Kris did the same. "They're making a run for it," she said, watching the van accelerate out of the lot. "Wimps!"

"I'll pursue," Max said, running to his truck. He suddenly stopped, seeing where the other shotgun blasts had gone. Both his rear tires had been flattened—shredded by the buckshot.

Kris, half a step behind him, grabbed his arm and tugged. "Come on. We'll take *my* truck!"

He raced after her. As she opened the driver's side door, he made a move to edge past her, but she jumped in ahead of him, waving the key in her hand. "Nobody drives my truck but me. Take shotgun."

"I've been trained in pursuit."

She gave him a level stare. "I've threaded my way through ambushes in a Humvee. You want them to get away while we debate our credentials? Go around."

Spitting out an oath, he raced to the other side and climbed in. "They headed east, toward Farmington," he said and pointed to the right.

She tossed him the phone. "Update the sheriff."

Showing restraint with the gas pedal, she didn't waste momentum spinning the tires in the gravel parking lot. Yet once she hit the pavement, Kris accelerated rapidly, going through the gears of the manual transmission like she'd been raised on high-performance engines. This was the old highway, two narrow lanes worn by decades of traffic, but she took the corners right on the center line, not wasting a single foot of road, yet staying in their lane—barely.

"Seat belt," she said, without looking over. He'd forgotten in the rush, but she hadn't.

He reached over and brought down the belt, snapping it in place. Glancing over, he could see they were going eighty-five, whipping around slower-moving traffic on the old road, now more of a country lane passing through the rural community of Waterflow. The van, a bluish-green Chevy, was in sight now, and they were closing the gap.

"Reach down beneath my seat," she said, "and grab my Beretta. I can't take my eyes off the road or my hands off the wheel right now."

He did as she'd asked, still trying to take in the fact that she was behind the wheel and doing some seriously skilled high-pursuit driving. The nine-millimeter pistol in a nylon tactical holster that was held high on the thigh was nearly identical to his own handgun. It would figure she'd make that choice, considering the military supplied a nearly identical weapon to its troops.

"It's got a key pad lock mechanism," she said, noticing he'd retrieved the weapon. She called out the numbers—the date of her induction into the Corps. "And in case you're wondering, I've got a concealed carry permit."

The road ahead rose sharply for a short distance, and humped up over an old irrigation canal. As they watched, the van left the ground slightly, brushing against the low branches of an ancient cottonwood. Dozens of golden leaves showered down onto the road.

"There's an elementary school ahead. What time is it?" she asked.

He looked at his watch. "Ten-thirty. The children should be inside, and the parents gone by now."

"Hope you're right. Those morons are going to be flying through a school zone at three times the limit." She eased off on the gas as the low, one-story cinder-block building came into view. "Where'd they go? I can't see the van."

"There!" He pointed. "They took a left on the side road. They're heading for the main highway."

She took the turn at forty-five, but the tires held, despite the squeal of protest. The van, obviously souped up, accelerated down the straight lane like a drag racer, widening the gap.

"That heap has some serious power," Max commented. "Once they get to the good roads they'll leave us in the dust."

The truck was going eighty, but they were still losing ground, and the four-lane highway was less than a half mile ahead. Max knew there was no entrance ramp, just a stoplight. "Think he'll try and run it? There's no way he'll make the turn."

"He still hasn't hit the brakes," Kris yelled. "He's gonna get hit for sure, or T-bone somebody."

Cursing, Kris let off on the gas, touched the brakes, then started gearing down, the transmission roaring in protest. The image ahead of them was surreal, like watching a train wreck about to occur, but in slow motion.

Finally the brake lights on the van flashed as red as the traffic signal. The vehicle fishtailed violently, then entered onto the highway. The van slipped right in front of a big SUV, forcing the driver to practically stand on his brakes, then the lucky pair whipped across three more lanes of traffic like a bullet, untouched. Max could hear the scream of tires from an eighth of a mile away, and blue smoke and dust filled the intersection.

"Hang on, it's gonna be close," she yelled as her pickup's brakes pulsed and stopped them cold after three sharp jerks. By the time it was all said and done, they were on the crosswalk, just feet from the stream of cars hurtling past in front of them. Cars continued to whiz by, although the SUV that had been nearly transfixed by the van had pulled over by the shoulder farther to the west.

The van, now racing up the hill toward an old natural gas plant, was nearly out of sight.

"Any way we can get across?" Max yelled, looking both ways and seeing nothing but traffic.

"Wanna run out there and blow a whistle? My truck and I will join you after the light changes."

He slammed his hand down hard on the dashboard and cursed, seeing that the van had disappeared. "Why did you insist on driving if you weren't willing to do what had to be done?"

"You would have played dodge car with *my* truck and *my* life? No way! I just saved both of our lives by not running that gauntlet. Instead of backseat driving you should be on the phone updating the police so they can pick up the chase."

He knew there weren't enough officers around to cut off every avenue of escape, but he called it in anyway, updating dispatch, then hung up. "We'll have to go to the sheriff's office and make a statement."

The light finally changed, and she turned right, heading toward Farmington, the closest community with a sheriff's department office.

Turning to glance at him, she saw that he'd placed the trigger lock back on her pistol and was returning it to its place beneath the seat. "Who were those guys, anyway? They can't be my enemies, so they must be yours."

Making a split-second decision, he decided she'd earned the right to know what was at stake. "Don't be so sure of anything, not at this point. I believe those men were connected to the theft of the platinum."

"The what?"

"The cargo, the merchandise, the stuff your sister and I were trying to deliver for the tribe. About a half-million dollars worth of jewelry-grade platinum was in that metal case, destined to be made into high-end jewelry by our craftsmen at the new tribal design facility." He met her gaze. "And that's for *your* ears only. The tribe doesn't want half the state of New Mexico running around looking for the stuff. We're searching for the raw material, not the finished designs. Tracing it would be impossible."

"Platinum is worth a lot more than gold, too. *Finally* you're giving me facts. So how about another? Why would those men come after us?" she demanded, as she continued driving east. "Or were they just after you? And if so, why?"

"Your sister hid the platinum before she died so it wouldn't fall into the wrong hands. I'm guessing those men were hoping we could lead them to it."

"I get it," she said, nodding slowly. "They want you, because you were there and knew my sister, and me, because they think I can second-guess her."

He didn't answer right away. "That's the way I see it," he said, after a beat.

His pause hadn't escaped her. He was holding something else back—there was another secret tied to the mystery that had claimed her sister's life. "There's more to your story. Tell me the rest or you're on your own from this point on."

"There *is* something else," he said, giving her a look of grudging admiration. "Your sister left a note, but only managed to get one word down—*Remember*—before she had to make a run for it," he said.

"Remember what?" Kris asked, mulling it over in her mind. "That's not much of a clue. Any idea what it means?"

"No, and that's why I came to you. I thought that maybe together we could figure things out."

"Was the note addressed to anyone in particular?"

"No, but at the time she probably thought I was either dead—or as good as. It would have made sense for her to have left that message for you."

"And she didn't address it because she was afraid that if Harris found it, he'd come after me?"

"That's one theory I've been tossing around," he admitted.

"And now you're thinking that Harris's partners found out about the note and that's why they came after us? If that's true, at least one of them must be working from the inside then."

He nodded. "That's what I was afraid of."

They rode in silence for the next several minutes, traffic

getting heavier as they approached the city of Farmington, the largest community in the area.

"There's something I need to know," Max said at last. "What would you have done if we'd actually caught up to them, and you'd learned that those men had been involved in your sister's death?"

"I would have done whatever was necessary to hold them for the police." She glanced at him, then back at the road. "If you're thinking I'd want revenge, you're wrong. I've seen enough tit-for-tat killings in the past two years. But those people made a big mistake. They came after *me*. And by doing that, they've ensured I'll go after them. When it comes to defending myself, I believe in being proactive."

Max considered what she'd said. He agreed with it and found his respect for her growing. "So what are you plans?" he asked.

"I'm going to finish this," Kris answered firmly. "I'm going to find the men who killed my sister and bring them in. After that, if the platinum still hasn't been found, I'll concentrate on finding it so I can return it to the tribe. I'm sure that's the way my sister would have liked me to honor her memory."

He said nothing for several long moments. Finally he spoke. "Police business is filled with ambiguous lines. If you choose to cross those lines, you better have a clear idea of what you're trying to do and how far you're willing to go to get what you want. Things can get very messy, believe me."

"Is that why you wanted to pursue them yourself?"

He regarded her silently for some time. She was smart and good at reading between the lines. Yet what he liked most about her was her confidence. She wouldn't take crap from anyone. A man would have a lot to measure up to before she let him get close, and that was the kind of challenge he thrived under. A sudden primitive need he hadn't counted on swept through him.

He forced himself to focus. This was no time to indulge in distractions—no matter how beautiful. "You just left a war zone," he said in a firm, reasonable tone. "To go after the man who killed your sister will put you right back into the line of fire. Are you really ready for this?"

"Yes, I am. I had hoped to leave the violence far behind me once and for all. But this is something I have to see through."

"These men will do just about anything to get what they want. You won't be able to lower your guard for even one second. If we continue together, I'll do my best to watch your back, but that's not a guarantee that nothing will happen to you." He waited, letting her consider the ramifications as they stopped at a light in Farmington.

"I have a question for you," she said at last. "Are you exclusively interested in going after the platinum, or does what happened to my sister play a part in your investigation, too?"

The question took him by surprise. He'd expected her to ask him about the risks, not his motives. "I was ordered to find the platinum, but I'll be doing both things at the same time. My partner, your sister, was my friend and I won't let that go."

They rode in silence the rest of the way. When they reached the sheriff's station, Max glanced over at her. "We'll get grilled hard by the officers. Be prepared."

"My answers will be simple and straightforward, unlike yours, I suppose."

"What do you mean?"

"Your history, your part in everything that's happened is…unclear," she said slowly. "If I were you, I'd work on keeping my answers short and generic. You're holding back information, Max, and any good officer will be able to pick up on that."

"Secrets are part of any operation—and of life, too," he answered, his voice somber.

Kris didn't respond. Like violence, secrets had been a part of the world she'd hoped to leave behind. Yet Max's world was obviously defined by secrets and seemed as essential as his own heartbeat.

When she glanced over at him she saw he'd trained his expression into one of total neutrality. Clearly, he hadn't liked the way she'd been able to read him, so he was making it much harder for her now.

The success of that effort told her something else about Max. Trouble and danger were sitting right next to her.

KRIS WATCHED DETECTIVE Lassiter of the Sheriff's Department stride around the small room, his face red and his lips tight. From his questions, it was clear the middle-aged, slightly pudgy detective believed that Max and she were part of a group of thieves who'd had a recent and deadly falling out.

Kris tapped her fingers on the table to the beat of a popular song playing only in her own mind, purposely throwing off his rhythm. He'd seriously ticked her off with his ridiculous allegations, and, trained to resist interrogations of all kinds, she was now making his life far more difficult.

"So," he demanded, "Any idea why these men would want to abduct you *and* Natoni? Had it been just you, I could have come up with a dozen reasons right off the bat. An attractive woman alone—plenty of motives there. But with Natoni involved, the picture shifts, especially with his recent history." He leaned forward, resting his arms on the table. "Make it easy on yourself. Come clean. This was a business deal gone wrong, wasn't it?"

"Some men jumped out of a van, and Mr. Natoni got tasered," she said in a cold voice. "They did a sloppy job so Mr. Natoni was able to help me fight back. They pulled guns on us, too, so I wasn't as concerned about their reasons as I was about mounting a good defense. I suppose it could have been an attempted carjacking or robbery since I'm the one who takes the receipts from my business to the bank. Either way, I'm a marine, and we make lousy victims."

"So you gave chase."

It hadn't been a question. "At the time it was a logical thing to do. Once we had them on the run, I figured we'd continue to monitor their location until your deputies could show up and take over. Our calls are on record, right?"

He didn't answer and began pacing around the room again. "Just back from the war zone, and looking for a little action to get the blood pumping again, eh?"

She struggled to keep her temper in check. "I saw enough conflict overseas, Detective. I came home hoping to find a pleasant routine I could settle into. But that's not the way it went down today, so I adapted."

He held her gaze. Then, at long last ostensibly satisfied with what he saw there, Lassiter nodded. "You and your sister were planning to run the nursery together?"

She shook her head. "Tina invested in the nursery, but she wasn't interested in actually growing and selling plants."

He took a seat and looked at his notes. "And you claim that this incident had nothing to do with your sister's murder?"

"I don't claim anything of the sort. *You're* the detective. I have no idea why those men came after us. All I can give you are the facts," she said, aware that he'd yet to mention anything about the platinum. "I've answered all your questions to the best of my ability, Detective Lassiter. Now I want some answers from you. *Why* was my sister killed? The police still haven't clarified that for me and I've got a right to know."

When he didn't answer her right away, she took another tack. "From your questions, it's clear that you think I'm somehow involved in what happened to Tina. So what harm is there in telling me the current theories floating around the Sheriff's Office?"

He leaned back in his chair, stared at some indeterminate spot across the room, then looked directly at her. "I've already helped you. I'm also a marine, a reservist. That's why I haven't come down even harder on you, Ms. Reynolds. A courtesy, if you will, so take it as a win."

She studied his expression. Lassiter's brow was furrowed,

his lips tight. He seemed to be at odds with himself. "And you also don't believe I'm guilty of anything," she said, taking a stab at it.

"Personal opinions don't count for much around here unless they're backed up with hard evidence," he answered. "But you're right, I can't see it. First, I knew your sister and I'm one-hundred-percent certain she handled herself with honor till the end."

"I appreciate your faith in Tina," she answered with heart-felt gratitude.

He met her gaze and held it. "Now I'm going to tell you the same thing I once told Tina. You've chosen real bad company. The Navajo man you're with left law enforcement a year or so ago, and, since then, his activities are a complete blank. He says he's working for the tribe, but nobody I've spoken to seems to know exactly what that means. Something's not right there." He paused as if intending to say more, but then just shook his head.

"What are you trying to tell me?" Kris inquired. "Do you think he had something to do with what happened to Tina?"

The detective hesitated. "Maybe he's a righteous guy, maybe not. But, one marine to another, check your six."

Kris recognized the jargon—watch your back. She nodded. "Count on it."

Lassiter stood, then walked out of the room, closing the door behind him. In the stillness that followed she could hear Max being questioned in the next room. Scarcely breathing, she made it a point to listen.

Chapter Three

"Come on, Natoni," Lassiter snapped. "Spill it. You figured to make a small fortune in platinum, but Harris double-crossed you and your partner. Though you walked out of the hospital, she ended up dead. Harris is also dead now, maybe run off the road by his remaining partner or partners, but what happened today suggests none of them managed to end up with the platinum. That's why the other members of the gang are coming after you. They think *you* know where it is. Tell me I'm not on the mark."

"John Harris is dead? You guys are sure of that?"

The detective gave Max an incredulous look. "The guy's toast. What's left of him is sitting in some cardboard box at the morgue. But here's the thing. Unless you come clean, you're likely to end up as dead as your partner. If I were you I'd spill my guts rather than have someone else do the job for me. Prison trumps death."

"Finding the reason those idiots tried to grab us is *your* job, Lassiter, not mine."

"You were a police officer once. What happened to you? Your word's sure not worth much these days."

Their gazes locked and the tension in the room escalated. He knew Lassiter was pushing his buttons. No one had ever believed how he'd solved his last case. Despite the life he'd managed to save his credibility had been compromised. But he had few regrets. That one incident had drawn him back to the Rez and made him who and what he was today. The "who" he could live with, but the "what" part of that equation still gave him more of a problem.

"You don't really expect me to believe that you have no idea who the men were?" Lassiter pressed.

Max paused for a fraction of a second, remembering the voice. He could have sworn it had been Harris's. Yet the police were convinced Harris had burned to death, trapped in his vehicle after running off a mountain road.

He'd heard a dead man…for all the sense that made.

"They were wearing masks and didn't exactly stop and introduce themselves," Max answered at last.

"What if I tell you that the woman's account of today's events doesn't match yours?"

"Then I'd say that you're either lying to me, or you need to take a closer look at your source. She just came back from overseas—deployed for over a year in a combat zone. That means she probably brought home a boatload of emotional baggage. No telling how many casualties she saw along those roads. Then just a few weeks after she gets stateside, her sister gets shot to death not fifty miles from home. You expect a calm, completely accurate story from her?"

"So you're saying that what happened at the nursery was the result of some penny-ante crooks looking to jack a car, not something connected to you two and the missing platinum?" Lassiter glared at him. "Coincidences are for fools, Natoni, and neither of us fits the mold. You're neck deep in whatever's going on. Come clean and save us both some time. Otherwise, we're going to be in here for a long, long time."

"Knock yourself out. I've told you all I know. Meanwhile, the bad guys are another mile down the road."

SHE'D LISTENED CAREFULLY and knew that there was a lot Max hadn't told the detective. For example, he'd never mentioned her gun. He hadn't lied, not from what she'd been able to tell. He just hadn't volunteered information, even when pushed.

The man was a pro—but at what? She needed more information. The problem was she had no way of getting it…except directly from him.

"Tina, what did you get me into?" she whispered in the silence.

A second later Detective Lassiter came back into the room. "Your attorney is here, and we're releasing you."

"My…what?"

"Tribal attorney Emily Largo is here."

"But—"

Before she could say anything more, a petite Navajo woman in a blue suit with long black hair tied back at the nape of her neck came into the room.

The woman made a faint gesture with the palm of her hand, indicating that Kris should withhold any more comments. "My client is free to go, correct?" It hadn't been a question as much as a statement.

"Absolutely. But we ask that she stay in the area," Lassiter said.

Kris looked directly at him. "My business is here, and so is every dime I have, Detective. Where else would I be?"

"You tell me," he answered.

"That's enough," Emily said, looking at Kris and shaking her head slightly. To emphasize the need to end this conversation, she gave Kris a gentle nudge out the door.

As they stepped out into the hall, Kris saw the tall redheaded man who worked for Jewelry Outlet. "Mr. Talbot," Kris said in a cold voice. *Now* she knew why he'd been coming around. He'd bought into the conspiracy angle as well.

"You may be leaving for now, but this isn't over," Talbot said. "The sheriff thinks you may be involved in the theft of tribal property, and so do I."

"Ignore him." Emily nudged her toward the side door. "Let's get out of here."

As they reached the exit, Emily stopped, then gave her a stern look. "I'm going to get Max. Wait here and speak to *no one* while I'm gone. Clear?"

"How much will I owe you for all this?" Kris asked, blurting out what was at the forefront of her mind. At the moment, her personal checking account wouldn't have bought two tanks of gasoline.

"It's already been covered," the Navajo woman said, then went down the hall.

Detective Lassiter joined her again as soon as Emily disappeared from view. "She's the tribe's top gun," he said. "Just remember my warning," he added, then hurried away.

A gazillion questions were going through her mind, but one stood above all the others. Just who exactly was Max Natoni? The guy had some serious connections, that's for sure. One way or another she'd have to figure out who she was dealing with.

Max came around the corner of the hall and joined her moments later. "Ready to go?"

"Yeah, they're through with me," she said. "But where's Ms. Largo?"

"She's got other business at the moment." He led the way outside. "I know you've got a lot of questions, I can see them in your eyes. But let's wait until we put some distance between us and this zoo."

She did as he asked. Neither spoke as she drove through the city and headed west, back toward the nursery, which lay between Farmington and the Navajo Nation along the San Juan River valley. Finally, after about fifteen minutes, he broke the silence.

"There's no turning back now. We're in too deep. You realize that, right?" he asked at last.

"I know we're both targets, yes. That also means I'm going

to have to stay away from the Smiling Cactus Nursery when it needs me most."

He nodded. "Otherwise you could endanger your employees or customers."

"I'll turn the reins over to Maria as soon as we arrive. She can take care of business for me until all the details surrounding my sister's death are settled."

"I think that's the right decision," he agreed.

Her insides were knotted but pride kept her voice cool. "Who are *you*, Max? I mean, really."

"I'm exactly who I've told you I am. I'm a tribal employee."

She shook her head. "There's more to you—and the job— than you're saying."

"That could be said about almost anyone," he replied with a slow smile. "There's more to you, too, than just being the owner of a plant nursery."

Max scarcely moved when he spoke. Like a good fighter, he didn't seem to believe in wasted motion. Yet there was a raw energy about him, an edginess, that made him exciting to be around. It was like watching the beginning of a storm.

"Talbot, from Jewelry Outlet, was at the station," she said, bringing her thoughts back into focus. "He thinks we're all part of the gang who heisted the platinum."

"Talbot's job is probably on the line. The insurance company doesn't want to shell out a bundle of cash to cover the tribe's claim and they're probably putting heat on Jewelry Outlet."

Kris rubbed her temple with one hand. "When I came back home I thought I'd finally be able to sleep in peace at night knowing I had a good chance of waking up again. That's all I wanted. But all I've found so far is more death."

"My people believe that when we restore the balance between good and evil, we walk in beauty," he said. "You'll find the peace you want once harmony is established again."

She lapsed into a long, thoughtful silence, then spoke. "Restoring that balance you spoke about is going to take a fight. The bad guys think we've got the answers, and the good guys think we're the bad guys. That doesn't leave us with many allies."

"Don't assume we're working alone just because you haven't seen our allies," he said in a quiet voice.

There was something oddly reassuring about his confidence. "*Who* are our allies?"

"The tribe, for one," he said. "We've got good friends who can be counted on to cover our flanks if things get hot."

"Tribal employees, like you? You're pretty sure of them?" she asked, her mind filled with even more questions.

"I am."

There'd been a finality to his tone that told her he'd answered all the questions he was going to for now.

As she glanced at Max she saw the way he held himself. His muscles were hard and tense. For a brief second she pictured herself running her hands gently over his arms and chest. Would he shudder at her touch, or would he be all hardness and control?

A delicious shiver touched her spine but, with effort, she suppressed it.

"You okay?" he asked. His eyes were dark and probing as they held hers.

Did his imagination misbehave, too, when he looked at her? She pushed the thought back firmly. Max Natoni *was* a dangerous man—to his enemies, and to any woman who didn't encase her heart in armor.

"I won't go back to work until this is resolved, but somehow I've got to make that clear to the ones who came after us. I have to make sure my staff stays safe," she said turning back to the business at hand.

"My guess is they'll keep a watch on the nursery for a few days and once they see you're not around, they'll pull out and go on the move. *We're* the ones they want. The cops will be coming around here often, too, now that the nursery's on their radar. That's company the guys after us will want to avoid."

Max's voice was low and smoky, a hunter on the prowl. Yet

in the confines of the car, it also seemed to hold an air of intimacy. She glanced over at him, then focused back on the road. *Smoldering.* That was the one word that best described him. So much lay just beneath the surface....

"You must really have some connections if you rate the tribe's top attorney," she said, mostly to see his reaction.

Max raised an eyebrow, then his lips curved in a wicked smile that made her breath catch in her throat.

"No answer?" she probed, refusing to let him get to her.

"As I told you, we have allies."

She pulled into her parking slot at the nursery. "I don't know what to make of you, Max," she said, honestly, "and I like to know the people who are by my side when I'm fighting. Overseas, the enemy generally didn't bother to differentiate between a combat unit and noncombat one. Knowing and trusting the people I was with kept me alive."

"I hear you."

He held her gaze for a second or two and she felt the impact of that look all through her body. Liars were usually polished, but there was a roughness to Max, an edge of raw masculine power that made her *want* to trust him.

"Your sister was a good judge of character," he said at last. "You know that. If you trusted her judgment, then you should also trust me."

She could almost feel the layers of secrets that surrounded him. "Let's take this one step at a time," she answered, then pointing ahead, added, "Does that have anything to do with your connections to the tribal president?"

Two Navajo men were working quickly to change the damaged tires on Max's truck. She recognized the name of the company on their jackets, too. It belonged to a nationally known racing team based in Farmington.

Following her gaze, he smiled. "Like I said, I have friends."

Again, a nonanswer. "I'm going to go talk to my staff and explain that I'll be away for a few days," she said.

"This operation may take much longer than that," he warned, opening his door.

"I'm optimistic," she answered.

"Go do what you have to, but hurry. We can't afford to hang around for too long. We're going to be under surveillance by the cops and the bad guys."

"All right. I'll meet you here at my truck in five minutes."

He shook his head. "You've got a great truck, but mine has a few extras that could come in handy. Bring your Beretta along with you, too, and the extra clips."

Kris watched him stride off. He was in superb physical condition...like an active duty soldier. In a way, maybe that was exactly what he was. What made Max Natoni even more dangerous was that underneath all the mystery that surrounded him beat the heart of one ultra sexy man.

Chapter Four

The Navajo man tightening lug nuts with an air hammer glanced up as Max approached. Turning the task over to his associate, a younger Navajo man who appeared to be just out of high school, he took Max aside.

"Thunder, *Hastiin Bigodii* wants an update," he said quietly.

Max looked at his cousin, Ranger Blueeyes. Under other circumstances, he would have greeted him as family, but an operation was underway and security procedures were required. The man before him now was simply Wind, just as he was Thunder—not Max Natoni.

Max told him about the voice he'd heard during the kidnapping attempt. "They were both wearing masks, but I'm one-hundred-percent positive that one of the men was Harris."

"John Harris is supposed to be dead. The authorities concluded that he drove over a cliff a few days after the theft of the platinum."

"The charred body found in the wreckage of Harris's car couldn't have been Harris's because he was here this morning, trying to kidnap the woman and me."

"Then it looks like we'll have to operate under the assumption that the man is still alive, no matter what the police have been led to believe. I'll pass that information along. Is the woman going to be a reliable asset?"

He knew what Wind meant. "I don't know her well enough yet to answer that. Her sister once told me that they were alike in all the ways that mattered, that there was a bond between them. But whether she'll be able to second-guess my old partner is something that remains to be seen." He sighed. "What complicates matters is that she doesn't really trust me. She's been trained to look past the surface. She's got an intelligence background in the military, so she's skeptical of halfway answers."

"Do whatever you have to do to get her complete trust."

"I'm working on it."

"If you're right about Harris being alive—"

"I am," he interrupted.

Wind nodded. "Then he'll come after her again. We've suspected that Harris had—has—a partner on the inside, so he probably already knows about the note. That could explain why she's become a target—and an asset that'll have to be protected."

"I haven't told her about Harris being alive, but she knows she's in danger. She's chosen to stay with me, but with her skills and training, she's more than capable of looking after herself."

Wind nodded. "Maybe so, but she's still an asset and it's our duty to guard her. The body count is high enough already."

"Harris killed my former partner. He won't touch this woman, not while I've got breath in my body," Max growled.

Wind nodded once. "I've got a source in the County Sheriff's Department. He said that Lassiter warned the woman—marine to marine—that your current activities are suspect."

"That could damage any seeds of trust that may have started to develop."

"Then handle it quickly, Thunder." Wind looked around for a second, then continued. "Have you tried…really tried…to use your gift? That could simplify things, stargazer, and put a quick end to at least one of the problems we're facing."

"I've tried, but nothing happened," he admitted. "So I'm

working on this case the only way I know for sure works—dealing with reality, not metaphysics. I'll get results."

Wind shrugged, then turned off the air compressor and began to help his assistant put the tools away.

Seeing Kris coming in his direction, Max went to meet her halfway. "Are you ready?" He looked at the oversize purse she was carrying—big enough to conceal her pistol.

She nodded. "I've done all I can do here for now. We need to plan our next move. How about if you take me to the exact spot where you and my sister first came under fire? Then I'd like you to go over every detail with me."

He nodded. "I plan to take you there and talk you through it, but first we need to shake off any possible surveillance."

"As soon as you're sure we're not being tailed, I'd also like to stop by my place so I can pick up a few changes of clothing. You can keep watch."

He drove down the highway in silence. Somehow he'd have to find a way to convince Kris that even though he guarded more than his share of secrets, he was worthy of her trust.

As the miles stretched out before them, he thought of Tina. "Your sister died doing the work she loved, Kris. She liked living on the edge and the job fit her like a glove. That may not be much consolation to you right now, but it will someday," he said somberly.

"Is that what keeps you in your line of work, the lure of danger?" she asked.

"Partly, yeah," he admitted. "I'd die by inches in a nine to five. But it's more than that. By working to restore the balance, I make a difference. That's the most any of us can ask for."

"I still don't understand your relationship with my sister. Neither of you was in the police force anymore, so how did you end up working together on this operation?"

"After she went freelance, I'd throw work her way as often as I could. I trusted her and she trusted me. In our line of work that's all that matters."

"Was there anything more between you other than work?"

"No," he answered flatly. "Not that your sister wasn't interesting or attractive to me." He took a deep breath and let it out slowly. He'd have to give Kris some glimpses into who he was as a man if he wanted her to trust him. "I'm not one for involvements, and neither was she—at least by that point in her life. If you're envisioning some sort of unspoken romantic attraction like you see on those TV cop shows, forget it. We stayed professional."

He paused, then grudgingly answered the question he could see still mirrored in her eyes. "Did I ever think about having a physical relationship with her? Sure I did. She was tempted, too, on occasion. If it hadn't been for our jobs, who knows what might have happened."

Kris got what he was saying. Tina had liked to keep work and play separate. Yet her sister had also often enjoyed uncommitted physical relationships with men. In that particular way, she and Tina were vastly different. Her heart would have to be engaged before anything serious could happen.

"Your sister's first love was her work and no matter what else you may hear, she died trying to complete her assignment. Before I'm through, everyone will know the truth, too. You have my word. It's a matter of honor—hers and mine. Do you understand?"

She nodded slowly. It was their mutual love and respect for Tina that bound them now. "At the moment, the note's your best lead, and I'm going to do my best to help you figure it out. With luck it'll also lead us to the ones responsible for her death."

They soon approached a familiar intersection and Kris sat up and pointed. "I live a short distance down that road."

"We can't stay long," he said, following her directions. "Pack quickly."

"After we leave my place, then what?" she asked.

"We'll go see a few people I know."

"I'm going to need more than that. I won't go into any situation blindly, no more than you would," she said, her voice firm. "I'd really like to trust you, Max, but you've got to give me a reason."

He understood her perfectly. He didn't trust easily, either. In that one way they were kindred souls. He glanced over at her. She was an incredibly attractive woman. A man could drown in those pale golden eyes. But what drew him to her went beyond that. He liked her code of honor and her loyalty to the people who mattered to her. Any man would be proud to have a woman like Kris by his side.

He stared at the road ahead, then continued. "Let me start by telling you something you don't know. I believe the man who killed your sister—John Harris—is still alive. I can't prove it, mind you, because I never saw his face, but he was one of the men who came after us at the nursery."

"Why didn't you tell me this before?" she demanded. "This changes everything. If Harris pulled the trigger and the police aren't even looking for him, I've got to do everything in my power to find him and bring him in. He'll have the answers I'll need to clear my sister's name. Harris *is* the answer."

"If I'm right, Kris, and he's alive, you won't have to go looking for him. He'll come after us with everything he's got. That's why he didn't care if I heard his voice. He intends to kidnap and force us to find the platinum for him. Then once that's done, he'll kill us."

"Let him come," she said, her voice trembling with emotion. "If he wants a fight, let's give him one he'll never forget."

Chapter Five

A short time later they arrived at her home, a faded green wood-framed farmhouse surrounded by an ancient apple orchard. He recognized Tina's car beneath a wooden carport, gathering dust.

Though he didn't say anything, it surprised him that Kris and Tina had moved in together. Tina had been a tough cop who showed the scars of coming face-to-face with the worst of human nature on a daily basis.

Kris, on the other hand, was cast from a different mold. Although she'd gone into what was one of the toughest branches of the military and had served a tour in a war zone, there was also a softer, gentler side to her. Despite the rigors of her former job she'd held on to that side of her nature, too. It was that duality that drew him to her, tempting him to cross the line.

Moments later, they entered the small home via a screened-in porch with a swing and several hardy-looking plants that seemed to be flourishing.

The floor of the old house was wood, the planks in good shape but worn down by decades of footsteps along the most common paths, especially through the doorways. It was simply decorated, with yellow curtains covering the white double hung windows, wallpaper in tiny yellow and blue flowers, and a braided oval rug in the center.

The living room held only a large leather sofa, matching

chair, and a mosaic coffee table. There was one painting on the wall of a young girl watching horses grazing. It was done in earth tones and, under the light from two tall floor lamps, had an almost mythical quality to it.

"I recognize the painting," he said. "Your sister showed it to me last year after she finished it—or at least a photo of it from her cell camera. She had a real eye for capturing people, though she never took herself seriously as an artist."

"That's because she never wanted it to become work— something to produce, sell or buy. Painting was her way of relaxing," Kris explained.

When she turned to look at him, he saw something else was weighing heavily on her. He waited for her to tell him what it was, but she hesitated, then turned and walked down the hall.

"I'm going to the bedroom to get my things," she called out to him a second later, never glancing back.

"Hurry," he said, moving over to the window to keep watch.

KRIS THREW SOME JEANS, changes of underwear and a few long-sleeved T-shirts into a small canvas bag. She could pack in a hurry. She'd done it so many times it was almost second nature to her.

She was still angry with Max for not telling her about Harris long before now. He was too good at keeping secrets, and that made him dangerous—ally or not.

She took a deep breath, then let it out again. Anger would only interfere with what they had to do. It was a luxury she couldn't afford, not when their lives were at stake.

She stared at the bag, then on impulse packed her duck-shaped slippers. They were undeniably silly looking, but they had a soft shearling interior that felt incredibly indulgent. She'd had them for years and they never failed to make her sigh when she slipped them on after a long day. Although she doubted she'd have occasion to wear them around Max, the slippers were her way of affirming that her life would be normal someday.

"Are you ready?" he called out from down the hall.

"Let's go," she said, coming out to meet him.

As they were getting into his truck, he glanced over at her. "I know you're still trying to decide whether to trust me or not, so I'd like you to keep something in mind. This is my turf, Kris," he said. "You've been away for several years and some things around here have changed, but I know this area like the back of my hand. Who and what I am can give us an edge—but you have to be willing to rely on me and my judgment. Any hesitation on your part may get us both killed."

"You're still not telling me everything. I know it and you know it." She held up one hand, stemming his protest. "Do *you* trust without reason?"

Max expelled his breath in a hiss as he started the truck's engine. "Okay. Good point. Both of us will have to work at this," he conceded.

"Your job's to get the platinum. I want Harris. That may place us in opposite camps somewhere down the line."

"Things have changed so you have nothing to worry about. I can't risk leading Harris to the platinum, so he's now my priority, too."

As soon as they were back on the road, heading west toward the Navajo Nation, she shifted in her seat. "Harris wants us, so why don't we use that to draw him in?"

He considered what she'd said and nodded. "That's a good plan, but we'd need some serious backup close by."

"We can manage it as long we cover each other's back." Seeing him hesitate, she challenged, "I can handle it, can't you?"

Her words were brave enough, but as he glanced over at her hands he saw her toying with her necklace. "No one's made of steel," he answered quietly.

"And here I thought you were," she teased with a hesitant smile.

He laughed. "Me? Nah. I just put on a good show, that's all," he said, eyes twinkling. "It's a survival thing I learned as a cop."

She laughed, knowing better. She'd seen him in a crisis situation. Although he felt pain and bled like everyone else, he had that toughness of spirit that defined a warrior.

"Hang on. I want to make sure we haven't picked up a tail," he said, suddenly making such a sharp turn off the highway that she had to grab onto the seat.

Max drove down the wide dirt road leading toward a tribal housing development, then made several detours and reverses. Finally they reached a solitary road parallel to the main highway. They were heading east again now, but the land was so flat and barren here they would have seen any vehicle attempting to follow them.

Twenty minutes later, he finally got back on the main highway. Traffic was heavy now, with many vehicles heading home at the end of the work day.

"Keep checking behind us," he said. "There's no one there now, but doesn't mean there couldn't be."

"I'll handle that. You take care of what's in front of us," she answered. "It's going to be dark in an hour or so. Where are we going?"

"Remember that souped-up van Harris and his partner were driving? I thought we'd go talk to people who specialize in those kinds of modifications. We need the type of shop that doesn't ask too many questions or keep regular hours. I have a source who might be able to tell us who fits the bill around this area."

After a short drive to the eastern outskirts of Farmington, Max pulled up into a parking slot outside the fenced-in garage that housed Birdsong Enterprises. A big garage bay was open, and several mechanics in blue overalls were working on a highly modified stock car behind another fence.

"What is this place? I see security cameras everywhere, and that fence must be twenty feet high."

"They don't advertise their location, but a relative of mine, Ranger—you saw him back at your nursery—works for the

Birdsong Racing Team. This is their local headquarters," he answered.

Ranger, wearing coveralls with "Blueeyes" embroidered above the pocket, came through the gate in the interior fence to meet them as they stepped out of Max's truck. The men nodded to each other but didn't shake hands.

Without preamble, and possibly because she was standing right there, Max asked Ranger about local performance shops with dubious reputations.

"The closest of these shops is a few miles farther down the highway, just outside Bloomfield, across the road from the cemetery and adjacent to the Wildcat Drilling Company's yard. The shop has a really bad reputation among serious independent repair shops, especially when it comes to their sources of used and rebuilt parts. The guy who owns it, Jerry Parson, has gotten busted several times for possession of stolen property. He seriously hates cops, so watch yourself." He cleared his throat. "A few months ago, some poor jerk tried to offer Parson some stolen headlights. He got mistaken for a cop and ended up on the banks of Farmington Reservoir, naked, unconscious and beaten half to death. He refused to press charges, but the story got out anyway."

Max nodded. "That's undoubtedly what Jerry wanted—the PR."

"You've heard of him?" Ranger asked.

"Sure, back when I was a police officer. But I never met him. Good thing, considering where I'm going next."

"There's a guy inside our shop who knows Parson well enough to give you some up-to-date background. You might want to talk to him before you set out." Ranger glanced at Kris. "It would be better if he went in alone, Ms. Reynolds. Joe won't say much around people he doesn't know."

"No problem," Kris answered, wondering how long ago Max had told Mr. Blueeyes her name.

MAX WENT INSIDE THE GARAGE. In an adjacent bay were two mechanics working on a high-performance carburetor. When he got closer, Max recognized one of the Navajo men, a warrior he'd previously known only as Smoke. His last name, embroidered on his work overalls, was Yazzie.

"I needed to get you away from the woman, Thunder," he said as Max joined him. "I have a message for you from *Hastiin Bigodii*. He recommends that you concentrate on Harris first, then the platinum."

"I agree. That's why our current plan is to draw him to us, make the collar, then worry about the recovery."

"*Hastiin Bigodii* also wanted me to remind you that if you need backup, help won't be far."

"Understood."

Smoke then handed Max a newspaper photo of Harris, not so much for him, but for Kris. Judging from the background it had probably been taken during the Police Athletic League's charity baseball game a few years ago.

Thanking him, Max walked back outside. Kris was already seated in his truck when he opened the door and slipped behind the wheel. "You understand the kind of place we're going into, right?" he asked.

"Yeah. Otherwise I'd have suggested we stop for dinner first. I'm starving, but I'd hate to get into a fight on a full stomach. I'm assuming we're liable to get jumped once we start asking questions, right?"

"That's the way I see it, but don't worry, I have a plan."

"I'm all ears."

After he filled her in, she said, "Okay. Let's go for it."

He was really beginning to like her. Instead of inundating him with questions about his plan, she was willing to play things out and roll with the punches. Before switching on the ignition, Max reached under the seat for his gun, removed it from the holster and stuck it into his waistband. It was uncomfortable there, but a holster was something a cop would have, not an amateur thief.

They were underway a short time later. Then less than a mile away from the shop, they stopped on a deserted road. Taking water from a bottle he had behind the seat, he prepared some sticky mud and smeared it over the plate, partially hiding the numbers and letters.

"This should work with our cover as amateurs," he said.

"Do these kinds of places—like the one we're going to—close at regular hours?" Seeing the surprised look he gave her, she added, "You know, to blend in."

"If they've got cars to work on, they'll be there."

A drilling company yard, with its stacks of drill casings and other heavy gear, nearly hid the old, converted gas station. They saw a cemetery and funeral home across the highway but almost drove past the garage before seeing the small sign that read Power House.

Max pulled in quickly and parked in front of a battered tow truck. Two sedans, probably belonging to the mechanics, were parked on the west side of the building, and a large blue pickup was on the east side.

There were four bays, one of which was open to the street. Two men were working on an old sedan, one gunning the engine while the other took a look beneath the hood. They could see shelves of auto parts taking up the far bay, and two more men were removing the tires from another sedan up on a lift.

"Here we go," Max said. "It's show time."

As they wandered toward the open bay, Max placed a casual arm around her shoulders. A spark of desire rippled through her from the close contact between their bodies. She pressed herself against his side, enjoying the warm sensations, and smiled at him.

"Making it look good as ordered," she whispered.

"I need to talk to the owner," Max yelled to one of the men, trying to be heard over the machine gun rattle of the air hammer being used to remove the car wheel nuts.

An overweight, heavily tattooed man wearing a dingy

white T-shirt came out of the office area, looked at Max, then gave Kris the once-over.

"Nice set of wheels, man," he said, glancing at the truck. "But we don't have parts for something like that."

"Not looking for parts, dude. I came to sell it—cheap," he said.

"Before the owner finds out, I'm guessing?" the man surmised, then gave Kris a longer look this time. "If your ole lady is nice to me, we might still be able to cut a deal."

"Watch your mouth," Max growled.

"Just playing with you, *dude*," the man said, putting his hands up in the air. "But tell me, what makes you think I'd be interested in a hot truck?"

"Hot? Hey, I just can't find where I put the papers, and I need some cash, you know? A guy I know said you'd do business without a bunch of questions, so how about five thousand? Cash," he added. "Heck, you could get twice that for the parts."

Max got a look at the last vehicle in the garage, a van that could have been the twin of the hopped-up job John Harris had used. He stepped forward for a closer look but the tattooed man he figured was Jerry Parson blocked him.

"You looking for a fight?" Max challenged, his gaze cold as granite.

The man laughed. "Hey, ease up, dude. Jerry's the name. That's all you need to know." He looked out the bay door at Max's truck. "You're offering me a good price," he said, considering it.

"That price is only good for someone who doesn't need any paperwork, or have any more questions."

"A few questions come with this deal. Gotta watch my own back," Jerry said.

Max suddenly realized that he couldn't see Kris anymore. Instinct told him that he had better keep Jerry's attention focused. "You're starting to sound like a cop now…. Wait a minute. Are you fronting for them? You wired?" he demanded loudly, looking around at the other employees.

As he moved around, feigning panic, he caught a glimpse of Kris inside the small office.

"Cops?" Jerry laughed loudly. "Us? Get serious!"

Max decided to enhance his paranoia up a notch. "That John guy, the one who was driving that same van earlier today," he said, pointing. "He's the one who sent me here. Bet he's a cop. Am I right?"

Kris reappeared at the side door near the office, and one of the mechanics spotted her immediately. She held up a half-eaten candy bar, smiled at him, then held it out to him. "Wanna bite?"

When the guy grabbed her by the arm instead, and pulled her close, she backhanded him with the knuckles of her free hand. Then, in a fluid follow-up, she reached down and pinched the nerve in his free hand, forcing him to his knees. Squealing with pain, he let go of her arm.

"*They're* the cops, boss," the man yelled, stepping back and giving her plenty of room. "See those moves?"

"Ex-marine, butthead," Kris shot back. "Every low-life who tries to paw me gets the same treatment."

Jerry blindsided Max with a jab to his ribs, nearly knocking him down. "They're just screw-ups, not cops," he answered, then stared hard at Max. "I don't know any Harris, and that van's a repo. You trying to jerk me around?"

Max stepped back and pulled out his pistol. "Back off!" he ordered, waving it around so everyone could see.

"Okay. You're cops," Jerry spat out.

"Wrong, Jerry," Max answered. "Which means you've really got a problem now. You shouldn't have ticked me off." He motioned for Kris to join him, then handed her his gun. He then grabbed Jerry, spun him around, and took the small pistol and holster he'd seen earlier at the small of the man's back.

"Keep everyone here, honey," he called out to Kris. "I'm going to see if they've got some cash we can take along— payment for our time."

"There won't be a hole deep enough for you to crawl into," Jerry growled.

"Go ahead, call the cops—if you want these photos sent to their Web site." Max used his cell phone and took photos of the garage, making sure to include every vehicle. "I'm willing to bet that a lot of this stuff's hot. And those license plates over there," he said, continuing to take pictures. "Where do they come from, anyway?"

Max rushed into the office seconds later. It wasn't hard to find Jerry's desk. There was only one. Pulling out the top drawer all the way, he checked inside, then looked below for anything taped to the bottom, but came up blank. What he needed was something—anything—that would give him information about whoever had sold Jerry the van.

He checked the desktop computer, trying to get into the software programs but it required a password, and he didn't have the time. He thought about removing the backup disk but discovered it wasn't there. Looking around, he discovered a DVD taped to the bottom of the middle desk drawer.

Max smiled, satisfied. He took the disk quickly and replaced it with one from the full box on top of the side table. Unless Jerry checked its contents, chances were he wouldn't discover the switch.

The entire process took less than three minutes. Grabbing all the cash in the box, Max hurried to join Kris, who still had his pistol aimed at the men. None of them had moved. Standing in front of Jerry and the others, Max split the bills into two stacks. He put one stack in his pocket and dropped the other on the floor. "Keep half, Jerry. I'm fair."

Not turning his back on the men, Max made his way to the truck, holding Jerry's pistol and covering Kris. At the last second, Max tossed Jerry's gun onto the flat roof of the garage, well out of reach.

They jumped into his truck almost simultaneously and raced off. Max kept glancing back in the rearview mirror as he continued down the road, then turned into a residential area, circling around so they'd be hidden from the highway. At long last he slowed, then stopped in front of a house with a For Sale sign that appeared unoccupied.

Kris brought a disk out from inside her blouse. "I've been trained to turn disadvantages into advantages. For example, if I'm outnumbered—they're slower, and I'm more mobile. With that in mind, I stepped into the next room, got a candy bar as cover and then snuck into the office. I didn't have a lot of time so I took the DVD that was in the computer—probably their backup disk."

He should have been angry, but he liked the way she'd taken the initiative. He brought out the DVD he'd managed to swipe and handed it to her. "This one was hidden—taped under the desk. Things turned out okay, but it would have helped if you'd have tipped me off ahead of time so I wouldn't have had to go postal to hold their attention."

"Concentrate on the results. We worked as smoothly as long-time partners. You picked up on my move and covered for me."

He nodded, then focused back on the road. She could handle herself in tough situations and improvise in a pinch. All in all, for a rookie, she wasn't half bad. And boy was she hot.

Maybe luck was on his side after all. "Let's take this as a win."

She shifted in her seat and looked directly at him. "Something else I wanted to point out. You heard Jerry make that little slip, didn't you?"

"Yeah. He said 'Harris' when all I'd mentioned was John. Now we *know* the van was his." He looked back at the road, trying not to smile. Kris was fast on the uptake and didn't miss a thing. He'd have to remember that from now on.

Chapter Six

Before long Max pulled to the side of the road. He picked up his pistol, which Kris had placed in the small console between their seats, returned it to its holster, then slid it back beneath his seat. "I need to make a call."

"To whom?" she asked.

"My boss needs an update from me. I'm going to step out of the truck so I can get better reception."

As he left the truck, Kris's gaze remained on Max. She liked watching him—the way he moved with an almost animal grace, the way he stood, feet braced, always ready for trouble. It was exciting just to be near him.

She smiled to herself, thinking that Tina would have approved of the attraction. Almost as quickly as it had formed, she squelched the thought. Her feelings for Max were just plain crazy. She knew almost nothing about him. Unlike most men she'd met, he never talked about himself. It was the ultimate in self-confidence, and that was part of the reason she found him so incredibly sexy.

She took a deep, steadying breath. This just wasn't like her. She was never this undisciplined, particularly not while on the job. And a job it was—for him and for her.

"Sis, I bet you're enjoying this," she whispered in the silence of the empty cab. "Wherever you are now, I bet you're laughing your fool head off."

Soon they were back on the road. As the miles swept past her window, silence stretched out between them. Finally, unable to stand it anymore, she spread her arms open. "So, are you going to tell me what's going on, or do we play twenty questions?"

"If we're going to play games I'm more a strip poker man, myself."

It took everything she had, but she forced herself not to even blink and she contented herself by staring holes through him.

"Okay, okay," he said. "Not even a tiny grin?" When her expression didn't change, he exhaled loudly. "Here's what I've got. The police are convinced that Harris is dead. They aren't bothering to speed up DNA or forensic tests on the body found inside Harris's car, which can take weeks anyway, because the physical features, like build and height, match. They also found Harris's college ring, watch and scorched wallet among the personal effects. As far as they're concerned Harris is dead, and *we're* their prime suspects. It'll probably be weeks before they discover the truth," he said. "Harris, being an ex-cop, knows how slow the state crime lab can be. I figure he counted on being dead for at least a month."

She checked the side mirror, watching for cars that could be tailing them, but they'd entered the city of Farmington and traffic made it hard to spot a tail. "Where are we going now?"

"To a dead drop so I can leave these two DVDs for someone else to study. Some programs can erase themselves if opened the wrong way, and I'm not good at that sort of thing. The computer itself had passwords, and Jerry has had plenty of encounters with the police before, so my guess is those data disks are encrypted."

While Kris enclosed the DVDs in the protective bag she'd found in the glove compartment, Max drove out of the city. After turning west and going several miles, he saw a flash off in the distance. It had only been a momentary brightness, but that told him that the Brotherhood was keeping a loose tail on them, using a parallel road. It also told him the dead drop was safe.

Max turned north, and before long they arrived at the drop point beside an old shack in the bosque, the forest near the San Juan River. Max parked, then walked to what had once been a sturdy wooden bench but was now nothing more than a few planks of wood. He placed the bag of DVDs they'd acquired into a big manila envelope that had been taped beneath the seat. Once finished, he returned to the truck and drove back east.

"You and I are going back to keep an eye on the chop shop," he said, anticipating her next question. "If Jerry recalls slipping up about Harris, he may decide to get rid of the van, or he might even contact Harris. That's what I'm hoping for— the chance to get to Harris before he gets to us."

"Sounds like a good plan," she agreed. "But tell me something. What was that you saw off to the north before you stopped at the drop point?" she asked. "Was it an all-clear signal to leave the disks?"

Max looked at her in surprise. He didn't give much away. He'd trained himself better than that.

"I happened to be looking at you at the time and saw recognition in your eyes," she added. "I didn't ask then because I could see you were concentrating. But I would like to know what you saw."

"Do you often look at me that closely? And, more importantly, do you like what you see?"

"*What* did you see?" she pressed, trying not to choke. "A signal mirror?"

"You're a hard woman to deal with," he chuckled.

She glared at him.

"I saw a flash that might have come from a mirror, like you suggested," he answered at last. "It was a sign that we've got friends around if we get into a jam. But don't expect instant help. That won't happen."

"So then you're not the only one who investigates on behalf of the tribal president," she concluded.

"No, but I am in charge of this case," he answered.

It was completely dark by the time they reached the vicinity of the Power House—Jerry's chop shop. Driving down the highway, they began searching for a good surveillance position.

"The cemetery's on higher ground and close enough for us to be able to keep a good watch on the place," she said as they drove down a dirt road adjacent to the grounds. "There are plenty of trees and shrubs there that'll give us cover if we need it, too."

"I was hoping for something else—maybe the old convenience store beside the highway. We can come up from this side, then climb up to the roof."

"It's doable, but a quick getaway would be almost impossible if we were spotted. The cemetery is a better bet." She paused for a moment. "Wait. I'm sorry. I forgot that your culture teaches you to avoid anything associated with the dead. I wasn't thinking."

He shook his head. "You're right about Navajo teachings, but the cemetery is a better location," he said, then turned and headed back.

Moments later, Max stopped beside the dirt road, placing the pickup between two cottonwoods to conceal the outline of the truck and hide the chrome as much as possible.

"There's a set of binoculars with night vision in the glove compartment," he said in a taut voice.

She pulled them out and used them for a moment to study the terrain, then handed them over to him. She could almost feel his tension as he took the binoculars, gripping them tightly. "You're not going to be comfortable here, staring across a graveyard, and the overall view from here isn't as good as I'd thought. Why don't we park over by the abandoned convenience store, like you suggested? As long as we stay on the east side, the headlights from passing cars won't illuminate us."

He placed the binoculars on the armrest between them. "That works for me. We can come up from the rear without showing ourselves along the way, and there's a big pile of tumbleweeds that'll give us some cover. We'll hide the pickup at the back of the building, of course."

A gravel road overgrown with weeds led to the old cinder block, flat-roofed store. After making sure that there were no transients in the vicinity, they took a position by the side of the building. From this angle and at this range they could even see inside the former gas station with regular binoculars.

Max scanned the area and spotted Jerry standing at the rear, beside the shelves, talking to a mechanic. "Jerry's the key player, so I'm going to focus on him."

Before he could say anything more, his cell phone started to vibrate. Max flipped it open with one hand and answered, "Speak."

The one-way conversation took several minutes. Max listened but gave nothing away. Finally he ended the call and looked over at Kris.

"The DVD you took was a backup of what was on the hard drive and apparently contained legitimate transactions recorded on the business software. But the other one, the one I found under the drawer, was encrypted. Since it's going to take a while longer to read, it's being copied. Both of the disks we took will be snuck back into Jerry's shop later and put back where they were. With a little luck, Jerry won't realize they were ever gone."

"Who gets the job of sneaking back into that place?"

He shrugged. "Not us."

She now knew for sure that Max was part of a much larger, specialized organization that included people with black-bag training. She was more determined than ever to learn more about him, but she still wasn't exactly sure how to go about it. Everything she knew about him so far assured her that it would be a challenge—but, then again, she'd always liked challenges.

He hadn't been looking at her, but almost as if he'd sensed

her change of mood, Max added, "We're on the same side. That's all you have to remember."

As Kris tried to recall everything Tina had told her about Max Natoni, she thought of one particular conversation. It had taken place after the close of a case her sister and Max had worked on together. In a somber voice Tina had assured her that the impossible was possible to Max—that nothing could ever be hidden from a gazer's eyes. At the time, she'd been absolutely certain that Tina had been downing too many margaritas in celebration. Now she wasn't so sure.

Kris brushed the memory aside for now. This wasn't the time for speculation—about what a "gazer" was, for instance. Bringing her thoughts back to their surveillance, she added, "What exactly are we watching for?"

"Harris will need another vehicle, and it's clear that Jerry has been dealing with him. Working with a man like Jerry, who has almost as much to lose with the police, would have made sense to him. Harris is in too deep to risk getting caught stealing a car," he said. "Harris's van is currently in Jerry's shop, probably destined to be stripped for parts. That's what makes me think one of the other cars being prepped has been earmarked for Harris."

"I'll spell you with the binoculars," she answered with a nod, "but I can still make out individuals, thanks to the lights around the garage."

"Tell me something. Would you have been at all uneasy had we stayed beside the cemetery?" he asked her after a beat. "Or if we had crossed the fence and gone inside, around the graves?"

"No," she answered quietly. "I don't believe the dead can hurt you. It's the living you have to watch out for."

"A few years ago I would have agreed with you whole-heartedly," he said, handing her the binoculars. "I've always been a man who believed in cold, hard facts only. But I've seen some things—stuff I couldn't explain in a million years. Let's just say I've learned to respect tribal beliefs, at least a lot more than I used to."

"Beliefs about the afterlife?"

He nodded. "Among other things."

"You mentioned once before that Navajos don't like to use the name of a person who has recently passed on. Why is that?"

"We believe that after death, the good in a man merges with universal harmony. The evil side remains earthbound and can create problems for the living. We don't use the name of the deceased because it calls the *chindi*, the evil side, something we do our best to avoid." He glanced at her, putting the binoculars down for a moment. "What do *you* believe?"

"I'm not at all sure about heaven and hell, not when people use them as addresses. But in here," she said pointing to her heart, "I know good people never die. Love is what defines them, and since that's spiritual it can never be destroyed."

He was no longer looking at Jerry's chop shop, but at her.

Feeling uneasy, she tore her gaze away and fastened the binoculars on their target. "What are you thinking?"

"That there are as many facets to you as there are in a diamond," he said in a low, husky voice. "You're a fascinating woman."

"Who can probably take you in hand-to-hand—so stay focused."

"Someday I'd like to see you give that a try," he said.

The rich masculine timber of his voice made her tingle all over, but before she could answer he called her attention to the door on the west wall.

"Somebody's coming out," he said.

"It's Jerry," she answered.

"He's getting into the tan four-door sedan," he said, after taking the binoculars from her and focusing them. "That car doesn't strike me as Jerry's type of wheels so let's go. We need to follow him."

They hurried back to the truck, and Kris jumped in the passenger's side as Max took the wheel.

"Let me guess," she said. "You see Jerry as the type who'd

drive that huge blue truck with the extended cab, the one on the other side?"

"Yeah, exactly. This sedan…it's eminently forgettable—the kind Harris would be interested in."

Max followed Jerry through town, and after a long circuitous route through the city streets, the sedan turned and entered a long, narrow, tree-lined lane barely wide enough for one vehicle at a time. Max followed, headlights turned off.

Located atop a low hill surrounded by housing developments was the city's oldest cemetery. The grounds had been poorly maintained, and tall weeds hid many of the headstones. The low stone wall encasing the grounds was tumbling down in places, and a large wooden cross atop a small rise had either been vandalized or been struck by lightning recently. It was charred at the top and leaning to one side.

"What's with this guy and graveyards?" Max muttered as he stopped his truck about fifty feet away. The trees on one side of the gently curved lane screened them from view, and the reduced public lighting there made the shadows deeper and darker.

"The driver got out," she said, having taken out the nightscope. "There's a second guy coming up to meet him, but I can't make out faces from here. There's no second vehicle in view, so our number-two man must have walked in from another direction."

They got out of Max's truck, leaving the doors open to avoid any loud noises. He'd turned off the dome lights long ago, so there wouldn't be any light to give them away, either. Moving silently and staying low, they walked slowly toward the men, angling for a better view.

"If we need a fast way out of here, there isn't one," Kris said suddenly. "We'd have to back up all the way down the lane. This smells like a trap."

"We can always duck into the trees and lose them in the cemetery," he whispered. "Wait for a bit and listen. Even if this is a trap, they'll still have to come to us."

"I'm getting a real bad feeling about this," she answered. "And what's wrong with that cross? It looks...strange."

"It was either set on fire or struck by lightning. If it's any consolation, it doesn't exactly put me at ease, either. The Navajo Way teaches that lightning-struck wood brings very bad luck and illness." Max then quickly put a finger to his lips and pointed back down the lane.

The men were walking in their direction. As they passed under a streetlamp, Max and Kris could see that one of them was holding a baseball bat, the other a crowbar.

Hearing the rustle of gravel behind them, they turned quickly and saw a large pickup pulling into the lane behind Max's truck, effectively blocking their exit.

"Jerry and his pal are closing in," Kris said, gesturing back to the parking lot. "We're going to have to fight our way out of this, but I'm not sure using our pistols is the way to go. If they're armed, too, we'll be caught in a crossfire."

They started moving back, working their way toward Max's truck. "You're right, guns are out unless they start shooting," he said in a harsh whisper. "Too many innocent people in the surrounding neighborhoods. And we don't want to bring the cops down on us, either."

"We're not going to make it out of here now that your truck's blocked," she warned. Then, as the men broke into a jog, she suddenly added, "They know where we are."

"They want to beat us to a pulp, which means we'll just have to be badder than the bad guys. Ever been jumped outside a bar?"

"Ever been a marine?" she countered.

"So, we go hand-to-hand and keep our handguns out of their reach," he said. "The hit I took on my side when they stole the platinum may slow me down, particularly since Jerry already took a poke at it tonight. But we have to take them on."

With their backs to Max's truck, they stood side-by-side, so they couldn't get attacked from behind.

Jerry was the closest to them now, the cross behind him in the distance, silhouetted in the setting moon.

Max wasn't sure if Jerry had picked this place on purpose, aware of the significance that lightning-struck wood and cemeteries had to a Navajo. Either way, he wouldn't let that be used against them now. Max braced himself, blocking out anything but the approaching threat. He could now see the other men coming up the lane, carrying crowbars or the equivalent.

"They'll try to take me on first," Max said, keeping his body square with Jerry's and the big man beside him. Both were wearing smiles and had raised their clubs to their waists.

"The big guy gets attacked first theory? If that's their plan, they have a surprise coming. They're about to get their butts kicked by a woman."

"Why wait?" With a loud war cry, Max lunged at Jerry, catching him completely by surprise. He landed a flying kick to Jerry's chest, hurling him back several feet. Jerry's wooden baseball bat flew out of his hand and landed farther down the road.

Kris lunged at Jerry's startled partner, who swung at her wildly with a crowbar, but she ducked and it missed her by a mile. Seeing an opening, she moved in close and punched her opponent in the throat.

The man gagged, stumbling back.

Seeing that she needed no help from him, Max whirled around and ran at the men coming up from the other side, yelling like a madman. Both men froze for a moment, but when Max closed in, one of them swung around a metal bat, trying to ward him off. Though he missed Max, the bat struck the man's partner, who cursed loudly.

Max spun, running back at Jerry, who was scrambling to his feet, still confused. Kris pressed her own attack, this time against the man with the sore throat, kicking him in the groin. He folded up like a flour tortilla, groaning deeply as he hit the ground.

The sound of a siren came from somewhere in the distance, then a second one joined in.

"Bail. We don't need the cops!" Jerry yelled, backing away. He pulled a small automatic from his belt and waved it in Max's direction while the other men hightailed it toward their vehicle, the one blocking the lane.

Max moved to his left, screening Kris from Jerry's gun. As he did, Jerry grabbed the arm of the man Kris had punched in the throat and hauled him along, back toward the cemetery.

"They're going to get away," Kris warned, stepping up beside Max. She'd brought out her Beretta, which was now down by her side.

"Let them go. Right now we've got to get out of here before the police arrive. And if these guys see us running, too, that'll help us maintain our bad guy cover." He jumped inside his truck and started the engine as she climbed in beside him.

Max started backing up, heading for the street. He had his lights on now, preferring speed rather than stealth.

"So who called the cops?" Kris wondered aloud.

"One of my friends probably saw the situation and gave us a hand," he said, seeing the thugs who'd blocked their way now pulling out into the street. "But if we don't get out of this area fast, we're going to be tied up for hours at the station."

When he reached the street, he did a smooth half turn, then headed down a side street. Seeing flashing lights ahead, he braked hard and pulled over to the side of the street, like any law-abiding driver. The police car flashed by, racing in the opposite direction.

"What now? Those men were our best lead to Harris," she said, looking in the rearview mirror toward the cemetery.

"You and I need some down time so we have to find a place to crash," he said, moving his shoulder and wincing. "This has been one heckuva long day."

Her heart went out to him, knowing he was in pain. Seeing anyone hurt was difficult enough, but Max wasn't just anyone to her, not anymore. Though he remained a riddle wrapped in a mystery, he was also her ally…and more. Refusing to define that further, she turned to look at him.

"Are you sure you're up to this?" she asked softly. "You're still healing from that round you took. Maybe you shouldn't be pushing yourself physically like this."

He nodded. "I won't lie to you. I'm not as good as new—not right now. I tire more easily, and my side hurts like hell. But if I didn't think I could do what has to be done, I wouldn't be here."

She understood what drove him—it was his allegiance to the Navajo tribe and his loyalty to her sister. Max was a man of principle and that gave her great comfort. Although she knew precious little about him, there were things one could expect from a man like him, and betrayal wasn't one of them.

"I know how much courage, and trust, it takes to admit physical limitations. It goes against the grain sometimes because we all learn to protect ourselves by never letting our guard down," she said gently. "If you want, pull off road and rest for a bit. I'll keep watch."

"Not yet, but I'll tell you this. I'm glad we're working together."

His voice was smoky and it drifted over her like a velvet caress. Just being with him made her feel things she'd never felt before—sensations she'd given up long ago as being nothing more than a creation of fairy tales.

"I'm going to make a call," he said. "Then we'll head to a safe house owned by some friends of mine."

"Business friends or personal?" When he didn't reply, she sighed in frustration. "You have way too many secrets," she said, then realized she'd spoken out loud.

"My secrets can't harm you," he answered quietly. "They're there to protect others as well as myself."

"*Trust* me. If there are no barriers between us, we could accomplish even more."

"Tell me what you'd like to get accomplished," he said, flashing her a devastating smile. "I'm sure we can work something out."

His voice was as smooth as single malt whiskey, and it drifted over her, warming her in ways she'd never dreamed anything could. With effort she focused.

"Stay on track. With people gunning for us we can't afford personal distractions," she said in a firm tone.

"Where we're going, we'll be safe. And we'll be able to talk there, too. I know you still have a lot of questions, and I'll answer as many as I can then. You have my word."

His voice was nothing more than a whisper filled with purpose, but she knew that he'd do as he'd said. If she was right about Max, he was a man who seldom promised anything, but when he did, his word was his bond.

Chapter Seven

An hour after Max's quick phone call, they arrived at a one-story log home in the foothills of the Chuska Mountains, west of Shiprock on the Navajo Nation. As their headlights illuminated the path ahead, Kris saw a house with a six-sided Hogan-shaped room on the left. Facing the front was a large bay window. A big dish antenna was mounted on the roof, along with a second array she recognized from her military experiences. It belonged to a sophisticated communications system.

Once Max parked, Kris stepped out of the truck and looked around. They were surrounded by a piñon and juniper forest, and, judging from the absence of lights, there were no other houses as far as the eye could see. On the reservation, at least away from the established communities, that wasn't an uncommon occurrence.

"This looks, at least in part, like the Navajo equivalent of an NSA site. Who lives here?" she asked.

"A friend."

"Why doesn't that answer surprise me?" she replied with a sigh.

As they stepped up to the porch, Kris saw an intricate, yet small, circular carving on the upper right-hand corner of the heavy wooden door frame. It looked like flames bounded inside a circle.

"What does that carving symbolize?" she asked, pointing. "It's not decorative, nor easily noticed unless you're used to looking for details."

He gave her an approving nod as he unlocked the massive door. "You're right. Most people wouldn't have noticed that at all."

Again a nonanswer. She shot him a dark look, then walked inside.

The hexagon-shaped room was cool and smelled vaguely of pine, a pleasant, homey scent. The walls and ceiling were finished in rough-cut lumber and peeled logs stained a rich brown, and the heavy curtains across the window were a rich turquoise. The ceiling beams all pointed to the high center, where a large stove pipe extended to the roof. In the center of the floor was a large cast-iron woodstove.

The flagstone floor was bare except for the large sheepskin rug between the front entrance and the stove. A simple square wooden table and four matching chairs had been placed by the large window.

"This is a beautiful home. Your friend must be well off."

He shook his head. "No, not really. This is a house he shares with others, like me."

"So this is your house, too?"

He shook his head. "The house belongs to the tribe. It's a place of safety for those who need it. That's all I can tell you. It's not my secret to share."

"I understand all about need-to-know and security clearance. But there *are* things I really need to know. We're working on this together, and my neck's on the line, too."

He didn't answer her. Instead he headed through an entryway into a tiny but well-furnished kitchen. He opened the refrigerator. "What are you hungry for?"

"What's inside?" she asked, her annoyance taking a backseat to a more pressing need—food—as she peered over his shoulder.

"Meat, cheese, veggies, ketchup, salsa, soft drinks. I'm going to make myself a sandwich and I suggest you do the same."

Spotting a breadbox on the counter, she brought out a golden, fragrant, circular loaf. She placed the surprisingly light bread onto a large oak cutting board, then brought it to the table. "I think it's freshly baked," she said, enjoying the aroma.

"Yes, it is," he said, sniffing the air and smiling contentedly. Then, as if suddenly catching a whiff of another wonderful scent, he turned and opened the oven door. "There's a huge pot of green chile stew in here. That, along with the bread, will make an excellent meal."

"It smells wonderful—like New Mexico, and home. You don't know how much I missed green chile overseas," she said, taking bowls from the cabinet. "And you know what they say, there's nothing like a good meal to help people talk."

He shook his head. "Too hungry to talk. Let's just eat for a while. There's a bread knife in the top drawer to the left of the dishwasher. And get a ladle, too, will you?"

Seeing the exhaustion on his face and remembering that he was still on the mend, she decided not to push him. She found the knife, a ladle and some spoons while he brought out the bowls. Soon they were both at the table, eating hungrily.

The stew was spicy, with the flavor of fresh, not canned chile, and the baked bread almost melted in her mouth.

They were close to finishing when she finally broke the silence between them. She'd been patient enough. "Is there anything you can tell me about your work?" she asked. "You already know about mine, and there'll be no...balance," she said using the term he'd used once, "unless you tell me a bit about yourself, too."

He nodded slowly as if in reluctant agreement. "What I do is a bit like law enforcement, but I follow different rules. I only work on things that directly affect our tribe, and require special handling in one way or another."

His gaze was direct and she had the feeling that he'd told her the truth—as much of it as he could, anyway.

"Do you ever find yourself dreaming of getting out of that line of work, of doing something else? Maybe something more…peaceful?"

"Like your plant nursery?" he asked with a smile. Seeing her nod, he shook his head. "The nursery has your heart, I can see that. But I'm doing the work I was meant to do."

"Law enforcement, of any kind, seems to take its toll on people," she said. "Tina slowly but surely became a world-class cynic."

"We see the worst in human nature day in and day out. That's what gets to you."

"She said something similar to me once. But I'll tell you what I discovered overseas. Even in the middle of the horrible chaos war creates, you can still see the best of human nature shining through. It's all in your perspective."

He nodded thoughtfully. "My people believe that good and evil coexist and a good Navajo should always work to restore the balance between them. That's what I try to do."

"That's a sensible way of looking at it, but you have to be careful not to let evil darken your outlook. That part's up to you, a choice you have to make daily."

"It's not really a matter of perspective. It's realism versus fantasy," he argued, shaking his head. "People like me prefer to deal with the facts."

"It's what's inside you that colors and shapes those facts."

"It's what's inside *you* that fascinates me. But I've got to say, the outside's definitely hot," he added, giving her a wicked smile.

Her skin tingled and a delicious shiver touched her spine, but, refusing to let him see how his words had teased her imagination, she laughed. "Flirting won't get you out of helping with the dishes."

Working together, they soon restored order to the kitchen.

"Do you want to rest first, or shall we have that talk you promised me?" she asked at last.

"Let's talk, but from the other room. I'd like to keep watch, and that front window will give us a good view of the area."

"If you open the curtains we'll be clear targets," she said, surprised that he'd even consider it.

"It's special glass. It would take an armor-piercing round to break through. But in either case, we won't be right in front of it, and we'll be keeping the lights low inside."

As she followed him into the hogan-shaped great room, she added, "Could we call the police for help from here?"

"Cell phone reception is tricky out here," he replied, taking a look outside. "There aren't many towers, with the low population density, and the terrain makes for a lot of dead zones. But here we're as safe as we can be until Harris is caught."

"All right, so let's talk," she said, sitting on the sofa. "Start by telling me this. Did my sister work for the tribal president in the same capacity you do?"

He sat down on the sofa with her and regarded her thoughtfully. "In a way. We would hire her from time to time."

"So she knew all about you?"

He shook his head. "Need to know, remember?" His eyes were calm and steady as they held hers. "I'm going to tell you more about what happened that day, but parts of this will be as difficult for you to hear as they will be for me to talk about."

"Go on," she said, bracing herself.

He took a deep breath. "Your sister made a run for it with the platinum that day because of me. After I'd pinned Harris down, I told her to take off. At that point I didn't know she'd also been hit, but she carried on despite that."

Kris's heart twisted up inside her and tears stung her eyes. As she looked at Max she could see the emotions flickering across his face—everything from rage to pain and disgust—but she didn't interrupt. He'd have to finish telling this in his own way and at his own speed.

"I was in the hospital when they told me she'd died. The round I took was nothing in comparison to the pain I felt then," he said, his eyes unfocused. "Your sister's body was found around midnight among an outcropping of rocks not far from the highway. She bled to death trying to do her job."

Kris had more questions, but the thought of Tina dying alone was almost too much for her to bear. Tears were rushing down her face. She stood and turned away from him so he couldn't see. Max came to her, but she shook her head. "Finish it," she said in as steady a voice as she could manage.

"There's not much more to say," he said, returning to his seat. "The police believe that Harris caught up to her on her way out, or when she ran out of gas."

"But you don't agree?" she asked, reading his tone. She was still facing away from him, trying to stop crying, but her tears just kept coming.

"Despite the bullet scars on the rocks around her, we don't believe Harris went after her. We think Harris pinned her down to keep her away while he searched the SUV. But then he was forced to take off when he heard another car coming up. There were tire tracks there that confirmed the presence of a witness, though the rain ruined the tread patterns."

She took a breath and swallowed. "*Who* was this witness? How come he couldn't give us more details?"

"The person who drove up, who reported hearing gunshots and finding the body, was a Navajo man who was out there gathering firewood. He raced to the closest place with a phone, a gas station down the road, then kept going. He was terrified of the *chindi*. He never left his name with the police, or told the clerk at the store who he was. So far, no one's been able to identify him, and all we know about him is second-hand via the store clerk."

Max tried to come closer to her again, but she moved away from him, still trying to compose herself and failing miserably.

"Do you blame me for her death?" he asked, his voice a strained whisper.

"No, it's Harris I blame. He killed her. You two were doing the best you could after being betrayed." She wanted to say more but the words wouldn't come. Sorrow welled up inside her, almost suffocating in its intensity. Taking a shaky breath, she continued. "What's ripping me up inside is that my sister died *alone.* That was what I'd feared the most for myself while I was serving overseas."

Ignoring her tears, she turned to face him, needing to make him understand. "Roadside bombs were killing more of our people than anything else. It didn't matter whether you were in a combat unit or not, you were still vulnerable. I had to travel those roads a lot and my greatest fear was that I'd end up trapped in my vehicle, and dying alone. It wasn't death that scared me—it was not having anyone who cared about me there to make my passing a little easier."

She brushed her tears away, trying to push back the rage and sorrow that were squeezing her heart. "I came home thinking that the worst was behind me, but my sister's death is my own nightmare come to life." Kris sobbed openly as pain seared through her in devastating waves.

Max put his arms around her. "We both lost someone we cared about. But we'll find justice." His hands skimmed over her back in the gentlest of caresses while he held her against him.

The heat of his body ribboned around her, reminding her that life couldn't…shouldn't…be wasted. In the safety of his embrace, life called to her, forcing the sorrow of death back for that one glorious moment.

She sighed softly and that sweet sound ignited his blood. Heat shot through his body as she pressed herself into him. He'd only meant to comfort her—an embrace rooted in compassion. He hadn't counted on his own body turning traitor. Greedy for more, he tightened his hold, gripping her buttocks and pulling her against the cradle of his thighs.

Tangled up in a web of need, he took her mouth, coaxing her to surrender to the passion between them.

Suddenly a brilliant flash and an ear-splitting crash shook the entire cabin, rattling the window. Kris ducked, reacting instinctively.

Max hurried over to the side of the window and looked outside.

"Just a close lightning strike," he confirmed. Unsatisfied needs still pounded through him, leaving him feeling on edge. "No rain, as usual, but lots of sound effects."

"I've never cared for thunder. It…unsettles me," she said.

He gave her a slow, sensual smile. "I could make you forget…."

The timber of his voice flowed over her, weaving past her defenses, making her feel vulnerable and fearless all at once.

Kris moved farther away from him, knowing she'd never be able to think clearly close to him. "We have to focus on Harris," she said firmly. "You can bet he's focusing on us."

He nodded. "You're right," he said. There was a dangerous, edgy darkness mirrored in his gaze. "Time to get back to work. Make yourself at home. There are a few things I need to do."

She watched him walk down the hall. He moved with purpose and raw power. She sighed wistfully. Max was like the sound of distant thunder over a parched desert—unsettling yet filled with unmistakable promise.

He glanced back, caught her watching him and suddenly grinned. "Doing a little recon?"

"I've just memorized all the basic terrain," she answered with a quirky smile.

With a low, throaty chuckle, he stepped inside one of the back rooms and disappeared from her view.

THE COMMUNICATIONS ROOM was accessed through the back of a bedroom closet. In a compartment behind a cork bulletin board was a stash of weapons, ammo and other emergency gear. Below that was a special laptop with encrypted files and a satellite phone. He also had a com link that would get him in touch with the Brotherhood, day or night.

He knew the layout of the safe houses well, having committed them to memory. This house had once belonged to a cousin of his and fellow warrior in the Brotherhood—but with a child on the way, he'd opted to live closer to Shiprock and its medical center.

Max knew he'd never marry. A career in law enforcement started out as something one did for a living, but sooner or later it became a part of who a person was. Viewpoints changed, quickly or slowly depending on one's experiences, and relationships often ended up as casualties.

Love required a leap of faith and blind trust, and he was incapable of both. He was enough of a realist to know that people invariably disappointed each other—and themselves. Love…it wasn't for him.

Kris had taken him by surprise, that's all. Hormones. Chemicals like that were designed to get a man in trouble.

Yet even as he reasoned it all out logically, a small voice at the back of his head warned him that he wasn't being honest with himself. What he'd felt…was more than that.

Shutting out those thoughts for now, he concentrated on the business at hand. Max entered his password on the laptop, then, once the system recognized his identity, he typed in an encrypted message. A response came in a matter of seconds as a coded series of letters flashed onscreen. Each letter corresponded to a number and, together, made up the telephone number of his contact. Max dialed it next.

Hastiin Bigodii answered. "What have you got for me?" he asked Max without preamble.

Max brought him up to date on the situation. "I'd like to intensify our efforts to find the Navajo man who discovered my partner's body."

"We've already done that. We've even left word with

area *hataaliis,* and if the man goes in to request a Sing, we'll hear about it."

"Maybe someone who lives in the vicinity of that store will know who he is or how to find him."

"We've got people checking at every home, but these matters will take time and patience. The Anglo woman...how is she handling this?"

"Her military training makes her a good ally in the field," he said. His thoughts suddenly drifted back to her softness and the way she'd pressed against him. Their bodies had fit into each other's naturally, as if it had been meant to be. Feeling his body harden, Max muttered a curse.

"Say again?" *Hastiin Bigodii* said.

"She has good instincts," he answered in a clear voice.

"The woman is a reliable asset then?" *Hastiin Bigodii* asked.

"She's a determined fighter because she has no choice, and wants to find the man who killed her sister."

"Revenge...that never brings anything good," he answered.

"It's not that. She wants justice and closure."

"Good," he answered, then continued. "I have some other news for you, Thunder. We decrypted the DVD you gave us. It contained a list of twenty cars, including two vans, one fitting the make and description you provided. Several vehicles were stripped for parts, others were sold as is."

"I think Harris must have arranged ahead of time to have a replacement vehicle waiting for him, knowing the van was going to be on the hot sheet after the attempted kidnapping. My guess is it's probably one of those listed as sold." He paused. "Can I have a copy of that list you mentioned? It's one lead I can use to track Harris down."

Names had power and using the name of an enemy was said to weaken him. Conversely, one never used the name of a friend if it could be avoided.

"It's on your computer now."

"*Ahéhee,*" he said, using the Navajo equivalent for thank you.

Max ended communications, then printed out the information. By the time he came out of the bedroom Kris was sitting at the desk in the den looking at the photo he'd been given of Harris.

"So this is John Harris?" she asked.

He nodded.

"Does Harris have any relatives in the area?"

"A cousin arranged by telephone to have the remains of the body believed to be Harris's cremated," he said, "but no one else has come forward. Why do you ask?"

"I was wondering about Harris's home. If he's assumed to be dead, what happened to his house? It's just sitting there, right, with the contents awaiting probate?"

"My information is that it's a rental, but the rent was paid up through the month. That means the landlord probably hasn't been able to retake possession, and the contents have to go through probate before the cousin can take them." After they exchanged looks, Max added, "I think the sheriff gave Harris's residence the once-over after the body was found, but the place hasn't been disturbed since."

"It sounds like a good place for Harris to hide, or at least go to for supplies like clothing, don't you think? He'd certainly have a key, and the landlord hasn't had a reason to change the locks yet." Her face brightened with anticipation. "I think we should go over there and take a look around. If nothing else, maybe he's left something behind that'll give us an idea of where he's hiding."

"We'd have to break in," he pointed out.

"You say puh-tato, I say puh-tahto. But look at it this way. Since he's alive, there's no reason to worry about the *chindi*. So what do you say?" she asked.

"I like the way you think," he said with a nod. "Okay, let's do it. We'll go right before dawn."

Chapter Eight

He watched Kris as she wandered restlessly around the semi-darkened front room. When the lamp suddenly flickered as thunder boomed nearby, she shuddered.

"Thunder is harmless. It's an echo of violence, nothing more," he said softly.

"But it's so loud up here close to the mountains. It sounds like artillery fire." She took a deep breath. "I guess I'm not adapting to civilian life as quickly as I thought I would. But then again, maybe that's a good thing. My senses will stay sharper and I need that edge now."

"Even without it, you'd still have me."

His voice reverberated with power. It wasn't bravado, but the quiet confidence of a proven warrior. She wanted to trust him...but she didn't even trust herself. In his arms she'd become someone else—a passionate woman filled with desire. She forced herself to stay focused. "So about Harris. We need to plan our operation."

"We'll have an opportunity to give the place a once-over before we make our move, but otherwise we'll have to play it by ear." He could see her start to protest, so he held up one hand. "If you preplan everything, you can end up making some bad choices. Trust me on this. I've been doing this kind of work for a long time."

She started to argue, then gave up on it. "So, you've had a past as a burglar, or was it a black-bag man?"

"You'd be surprised what's in my past," he answered with a grin.

"Somehow, I don't think I would be," she answered, then, looking at the page in his hand, continued. "What have you got?"

He showed her the list of cars and explained what they were. "I've circled four of these as possible models Harris might have chosen as replacements for his van."

She studied the list. "The ones you've marked are all white or cream colored, and they're all four doors, mid-range, or economy sedans."

"Yeah—nondescript, generic looking and very forgettable. That's why I think he would have chosen one of those models," he said.

She nodded. "What of the Navajo man you told me about, the one who found my sister? I know you mentioned that fear of the *chindi* could have sent him almost anywhere."

"Others are working on that," he said.

"Your tribal friends?"

"Colleagues," he nodded.

She paused. "Those colleagues...do they have something to do with the circle of fire carved into the entrance?"

The way she put things together so quickly never ceased to surprise him, but he did his best to cover his reaction. He shrugged in response, knowing that was better than no reaction at all, since Kris would have read too much into a nonanswer.

"Will you ever tell me who you really are?" she probed.

"You know all you need to already. I'm your ally," he answered, then stopped as a curious buzz came from what looked like a heater vent. "That's the satellite phone. I'll be right back."

She watched him leave. He was like approaching thunder mingled with the brush of rain on a summer night. How could one man embody both gentleness and violence all in one? All she knew for sure was that Max Natoni remained a mystery couched in shadows.

HE HURRIED INTO THE ROOM so quickly, the door didn't completely shut behind him. He knew that the phone wouldn't have been ringing unless it was urgent.

"This is Thunder," he said, answering.

It was *Hastiin Bigodii.* "We've just learned something that's crucial to your investigation, Thunder," he said. "Harris's dental records match what was found on the charred body. Are you *sure* you heard his voice?"

"I am," he said. "Harris is alive."

"Dental records don't lie."

"Then he faked it somehow, or got to the records. I heard his voice," he repeated flatly. "There's no mistake. Do you have that report? I'd like the details."

"All I got was the medical examiner's summary. It's now up to you to decide how to use this information," *Hastiin Bigodii* answered.

"Understood."

SHE'D CASUALLY FOLLOWED HIM down the hall and had stopped just outside the partially open bedroom door, listening. His code name, Thunder, fit him perfectly. Hearing his conversation come to an end, Kris edged back silently, intending to hurry back before she gave herself away.

She'd gone only a few feet when Max suddenly came out into the hall. He'd taken off his jacket, and since the top buttons of his shirt had fallen off somewhere along the way, it now hung halfway open. He looked so wonderfully male, Kris felt her breath catch. As they stood face-to-face, she was suddenly at a loss for words.

He closed the door behind him. Then, as if sensing her response to him, Max stepped closer to her. Kris, aware of him in ways that made her knees weak, took several quick steps back but ran into the wall.

Holding her gaze, he stepped closer to her again. "Something you need from me?" he asked huskily.

She raised her hand to push him back, but as she touched his chest, desire thrummed through her. "I just came over to see if I could help," she managed. It was lame—very lame—but she couldn't think of anything else.

"Try again, darling," he said, bracing his arms against the wall and pinning her between them. "You were hoping to find out who was calling me...and more?" he asked in a rough, masculine drawl.

Her mouth went dry. "Thunder...that's your code name? Code names aren't used in police work, not unless you're undercover. So what are you part of—Homeland Security?"

"In a way," he answered. He was a patriotic American, but the Navajo Nation was *his* homeland.

She ducked under one of his arms and quickly put more distance between them. "Can I come in and take a look at your setup? I'm very familiar with communications systems. In a pinch, I could call for help if you're otherwise occupied."

He considered it for several long moments. "All right. I trust you, and this is one way to prove it. But before you come in, I want your word that you'll never discuss what you see with anyone else. This has to remain between us."

"You have my word," she said, her heart hammering with excitement. She had to find out everything she could about Max Natoni, the only man who'd ever made her blood sing.

He led her through the closet into the communications room and showed her the layout. "We're not alone in this. I told you before, but now you've got reason to believe me."

The arsenal he had available told her he wasn't just a courier or high-paid security. Instinct assured her that there was a lot more to Max Natoni than she'd ever dreamed, but Kris also knew she wouldn't get anything more out of him—at least not tonight.

After a good look around, she took her cue from him and stepped out into the hall. "Thanks for showing this to me. Your trust…means a lot."

"You're welcome, but remember our agreement," he said, shutting the door behind them.

"I will."

"I want to get to Harris's place before daybreak, so we'll set out at four in the morning," he said.

"Sounds like a good time. Even if he's there, he's not likely to be awake."

"That's why so many departmental raids happen early in the morning," he said.

"And tonight we stay here, right?"

"Yes. This is the safest place for us." He led her down the hall to a simply furnished bedroom. "Your bag's in here already, and there are blankets in the closet if you need them. But there are other ways to stay warm," he said, his gaze burning through her.

Max was offering her the chance to share his bed and she ached to say yes. Instinct told her that dark pleasures awaited her in his arms and it took all she had not to take him up on his offer.

"This room will do just fine. Thank you." Although he didn't move a muscle, she saw the flicker of disappointment that flashed in his eyes.

"Then sleep well. I'll wake you up at three and we'll get ready."

As he walked away, the temptation to ask him to come back clawed at her. It was then that she realized just how dangerous Max truly was.

Although she soon crawled into bed, Kris had a hard time falling asleep. The rumble of thunder outside made her uneasy. Tossing the covers back, she reached into her canvas bag and brought out her comfortable and well-worn duck slippers. The soft feel of shearling on the inside of each felt familiar and comforting. It wouldn't replace the pleasures Max had offered her, but there was sure something to be said for this, too.

Kris walked to the bookshelf and found a book about life on the reservation during the early nineteenth century. Hours later, she drifted off to sleep, her dreams haunted by a man who commanded the silent mysteries of the desert night.

IT WAS STILL DARK when Kris heard a light rap on her door. She bolted to her feet, instantly awake, her hand on her Beretta, which was on the nightstand.

"We leave in fifteen," Max said, then the sound of his footsteps faded down the hall.

She'd never be able to sleep deeply until they finished what they'd set out to do. Fully awake, she got ready in less than ten minutes, combing her hair and tying it back in a ponytail, then packing everything away. As she stepped into the living room, Max handed her a cup of freshly brewed coffee. It smelled wonderful.

Kris noticed that he had several extra clips of ammo on his belt beneath his jacket, opposite his pistol holster. "I have my Beretta and an extra clip, which I'll keep in a jacket pocket," she said. "Do you want to me to carry anything else?"

He shook his head. "I've got that covered, but the truth of it is we can't fire a weapon inside the city—not unless we have absolutely no other choice."

"Then it's hand-to-hand if we get into a jam. We can handle that."

He threw her a collapsible metal baton. "Ever use one of these? They can come in handy."

"We were trained in a variety of fighting techniques. I can use this effectively," she said, demonstrating by extending the baton to full length, then collapsing it again quickly.

They were underway less than fifteen minutes later, and she

used the light coming from the instrument panel to examine the list of cars he'd brought with him.

"I'll keep an eye out for the models you picked out. If I see any of them, I'll let you know. With luck, we'll run into Harris today. But don't worry. I'll be happy to turn him over to you once he and I get…acquainted."

"I've given this some more thought and I don't think it's likely he'll be there at the house," Max said. "He's worked hard to make the police believe he's dead, so I doubt he'd risk being seen by a neighbor at this stage of the game."

"That all depends on how close the houses are where he lives, doesn't it? And being an ex-cop, he may figure now would be the best time to go in or come out, when most of the world's asleep."

He shrugged. "We'll see."

They entered the modest residential neighborhood off Hutton Avenue in Farmington's east side about fifty minutes later. It was a few minutes past four in the morning, cold and quiet, and the streets were all but deserted. Max kept an eye out for dogs, and listened, but could hear nothing except the soft hum of his pickup's engine.

He circled the general neighborhood twice before going down Harris's street, thinking that the man would have been more likely to park one or two blocks away, then walk over to his house. Although they both searched for any car that matched the ones on the list, none did.

As they drew near Harris's home, Max noticed a police cruiser parked two houses down from the front door. It wasn't a marked car, but the antennae and state plates were dead giveaways.

He pointed out the officer and car to Kris, then cruised past slowly, making sure not to make eye contact with the officer inside. "FPD is playing it safe. Despite what local law enforcement has been saying publicly, at least the Farmington cops aren't totally convinced that Harris is dead. Otherwise, that car wouldn't have been there."

"Should we abandon our plans to search the place?"

"No, but we'll have to gain entrance through the back. It's still risky, though. If the officer changes position and spots us, we're in a world of trouble. You still game?"

She considered it for a moment, then nodded. "I'm in."

"Good. There's a utility easement at the rear of the property wide enough for trucks. This time of night, it's not likely that neighbors will be up and looking out, but dogs are a different matter." He cast a sharp look her way. "If one of them starts barking and won't let up, someone's going to take a look. If that happens we cut and run. Understood?"

"Perfectly."

They parked at the end of the block, behind another vehicle and two houses away from Harris's rental house—easily identifiable because of the For Rent sign outside.

Max slipped on gloves and waited for her to do the same. Together, they crept forward silently, using the long shadows from trees and outbuildings that lined the alley as cover. Passing the first backyard, she saw what was obviously a productive garden during the growing season. The remnants of a few rows of corn remained, and she could see big pumpkins on their vines, ripening up for days ahead.

Yet, try as she might, in comparison to him, she sounded like an elephant walking over a bed of peanuts. Absolutely everything she stepped on seemed to crunch beneath her feet, from fine gravel to dried-out weeds.

Max never glanced back at her, nor showed any annoyance, so maybe it wasn't as bad as it sounded to her. She kept up with him while still watching their six.

When they reached the rear of the property, they followed the field fence line to a wood-framed wire gate. Max froze, signaled for her to do the same, and listened.

She'd always had very good hearing and now, as she focused on the sounds, she made out a few crickets who hadn't gone into survival mode yet, but not much else. A dog was barking off in the distance but none were nearby. She could hear the rumble of traffic just beyond the neighborhood streets, and the faint electronic buzz of a transformer on a power pole at the end of the property line about twenty feet away.

The gate had a screen door-type latch, and within fifteen seconds they were standing beneath the overhang of a small back porch. The screen door was unlocked, and the entry door was solid, metal-clad wood, designed to deter a simple smash and grab.

Marines were taught how to kick in a door or blow it off the hinges, but obviously something with a little more subtlety was needed here. She saw Max remove a jagged-looking house key from his pocket, along with a small rubber hammer. "Lock bumping," he whispered. "Works fast. Once we leave, everything will look exactly the way it was before we broke in."

The process was amazingly simple, and the dead bolt was defeated in the same fashion. Max swung open the door, and as they stepped inside Kris switched on her small penlight. When they advanced, Kris saw that Max had his weapon out. If they'd managed to elude the police officer outside, it was possible Harris had, too.

They passed through the kitchen quickly, working as a team, and inspected the rest of the house room by room. Satisfied at last that they were alone, he put his pistol away.

"Search for anything that might tell us where Harris has gone. But put everything back exactly where you found it," Max murmured softly. "We don't want to leave any traces that we were here. The house is probably still sealed pending legal issues."

"If he left no will…" She remembered being warned about those legalities, but she'd known that Tina had kept hers with the attorney they'd both consulted. Tina's will had been as simple as her own—if either of them died, everything went to the other. Not that there'd been a lot for either of them to leave behind.

As Kris moved into the study, moonlight was streaming between the part in the curtains. The light covering of dust on the hardwood floor revealed a man's footprints. The tread pattern was distinctive. One heel had an angular cut across it.

Kris stepped out into the hall and signaled to Max. He left the drawer he'd been searching and came over to study the footprints. "It's the sole of a size twelve or so hunting boot available at sporting goods stores. I recognize the logo. I'll go through the shoes and other items in his closet and see if I can find any other gear from that company."

Kris started searching through the office trash can next, while Max went down the hall to the master bedroom. Several of the envelopes were unopened and, from the Statement Enclosed message on each, contained bills. It was clear that Harris hadn't planned on being around to pay them.

Following a hunch, Kris went to the window to check on the cop outside. As she did, Max came into the room.

"Nothing in his closet matches those boot prints," he said, "which reinforces the possibility that Harris has been here since his supposed death."

"The officer across the street is starting to get restless," she warned. "He's out of his car and walking around."

"Maybe he's a rookie and drank too much coffee, or he's going to make a routine check of the back. We left everything undisturbed and locked, so he won't find anything wrong if he checks the back door. Just stay low and be careful with the penlight. And let's finish up quickly. What have you got so far?"

"Lots of unopened bills. I was thinking of checking the ones from the credit card companies next."

"Good. While you're working on that, I'll take the filing cabinet."

Seeing one folder labeled Dentist, Max pulled it out and soon found a bill for a duplicate set of dentures. He smiled slowly. Harris had needed the extra set because he'd planned to place the first set with the victim of his staged auto crash. That's why the police had been able to match dental records. No telling *who* the body had really belonged to at this point.

Just to test out his theory, he went to the bathroom and checked for a second set on the vanity or the medicine cabinet. He searched the bedroom next but found nothing.

When he came back into the study, Kris had already identified credit card purchases from several stores, including Harley's Sporting Goods and the Fishing Hole near Navajo Lake.

"He bought a tent and a lot of camping gear a little over two weeks ago," Kris said. "The items are abbreviated, but I can make them out, especially on this big discount store's statement. And here's something from that Harley's Sporting Goods, a pair of size 12 boots. Is this the brand?" She showed him the item on the statement.

"Sure is. That's about the same time he got the news that he'd be part of the escort team that would travel with the platinum," he said.

She nodded. "You couldn't find the boots, so let's take a quick look around for the tent and gear. If they're not here either, then he's using them now."

After searching and finding no trace of the camping equipment, they left silently and returned to his truck. Max was about to switch on the ignition when he saw Harris's neighbor, the one at the end of the block, coming out of his front door carrying a tackle box and two fishing rods.

"You think maybe he's going to hook up with Harris?" Kris whispered.

"Bad pun," he said with a grin, "but maybe. Let's follow him and see where he takes us. The early bird catches the worm."

Chapter Nine

The man loaded up more gear, then climbed into his pickup and pulled out of the driveway. They followed at a discreet distance, an easy task with so few vehicles on the road. About five minutes later, the man pulled into a coffee shop beside Browning Parkway. Even though it was barely five-thirty and sunrise still more than an hour away, the parking lot was already crowded.

They went inside and, following the man's lead, found a spot at the counter, next to him.

"Look's like you're taking the day off," Max commented offhandedly, pointing to the man's well-worn fishing vest. It had a few lures attached—mostly trout flies—and a distinctive earthy scent.

"Every day's my day off now, young fellow. Gonna spend a few days up at Navajo Lake," he answered, running one hand through his thinning grey hair. "Nothing like time alone to think."

"Have we met before?" Max asked. "You look familiar."

The man studied Max's face, then shook his head. "Can't say I remember you."

Max pretended to mull it over. "Wait…I know where I've seen you before. You're John Harris's neighbor, aren't you? Like him, I used to work for the police department, and I've seen you outside in your backyard a few times when I've gone over there."

The man smiled. "I do a lot of gardening. It helps keep my blood pressure down. Greg Mullins' the name." Greg didn't offer to shake hands, undoubtedly aware that Navajos disliked casual physical contact with strangers.

Noticing that Greg seemed more relaxed now, Max ordered some doughnuts and coffee for him and Kris. As soon as the waitress moved away, Max continued. "I tried several times to get John to go fishing, but he was never interested. Or maybe he just didn't want to go and get shown up."

The man laughed. "I don't think he was much of an out-doorsman. Just a few days before he had that accident, I saw him out in his backyard, trying to figure out how to pitch a tent. He was having one heckuva time with it," he said, chuckling. "Maybe he was planning on taking you up on the fishing offer but wanted to get some experience first. No need for a tent unless you plan on staying overnight." Greg stared at his coffee absently. "That's why I'm heading off now. You never know when your ticket's going to get punched."

After filling his Thermos with fresh coffee, Greg was on his way. Kris and Max followed him out a few minutes later.

"That was a great breakfast," Kris said, finishing the last of her doughnut after fastening her seat belt. "It covered all the major food groups—sugar, flour, lard and caffeine."

He laughed. "Let's go pay a visit to those sporting goods stores we found receipts for and see what we can find out. Maybe someone will remember Harris."

"And if someone asks why you want to know?"

"I'll say that I'm a P.I. looking into his death."

She nodded. "Okay, and I'm your partner."

"I was thinking of assistant."

"Partner, or you can stuff it."

"Partner it is," he said, laughing. "Let's go to the mall first. They stay open 24/7, and that's where he bought the sleeping bag."

Unable to find the clerk who had sold the item to Harris, and, since it was too early to check the other stores, they parked in a local hospital parking lot. It was an unlikely but relatively safe spot to hide "in plain sight." There, they took turns catnapping. Yesterday had been endless, and both were grateful for the opportunity to get another hour or so of sleep.

They arrived at Harley's Sporting Goods at nine o'clock sharp. The parking lot in front of the low-profile cinder-block building was empty. Max parked under the shade of a tall maple, which still had leaves, though most had turned shades of brown and gold. "Looks like the owner works on Indian time," he said with a chuckle, pointing out the running joke about his tribe's lack of interest in Anglo schedules. "We'll have to wait a few more minutes."

She squinted and looked toward the store. The windows were protected with wrought-iron security bars, but she finally found a sign. "It doesn't open until nine-thirty."

He smiled. "Then we're on Anglo time—early."

In the close confines of the truck she was too aware of everything about him. Max had shifted and was leaning against the driver's side door. Several buttons of his shirt were undone. Beneath, he was all muscle and bronzed skin, enough to make any sane woman drool. Though her heart was doing a frantic dance, he seemed completely relaxed and totally unaware of how he was affecting her. It took all her willpower not to sigh. She looked around, searching for a distraction.

He shifted then and, moving slowly, leaned toward her. For one crazy moment she thought he was about to kiss her. Instead, he cupped a small butterfly that had landed on her shoulder, and released it out the car window.

Kris, suddenly aware that she'd been holding her breath, tried not to do anything obvious like gulp in air. "That wasn't a bad passenger to carry. She could have stayed. Probably one of the last of the season."

"Butterflies belong outside, enjoying their freedom. To walk in beauty you have to realize that everything has its proper place."

"When you say things like that, I can feel how close you are to your tribe. But at other times, I get the feeling that there's a wide gulf between your personal beliefs and those of Navajo traditionalists," she said, then looked at him, hoping he'd tell her more about himself.

"I left the reservation when I was in my teens and grew up on the outside—living on Anglo time," he answered. "I'm a product of two cultures and my beliefs reflect that. That's why I only accept things to a certain point." As he glanced down at the medicine bag he wore, his fists balled up, but then he forced himself to relax again.

She was about to ask him why he always wore the medicine pouch if he didn't trust things that couldn't be empirically proven, but Max suddenly sat up straight.

"Here comes someone now," he said.

They saw an Anglo man in his early fifties wearing a green Henley shirt, leather vest and jeans park his pickup near the entrance. He looked them over carefully, nodded, then unlocked the heavy iron security door and the door it was protecting. The proprietor was wearing what looked like a Colt .45 revolver in a Western-style holster, not surprising considering that the business also sold firearms.

"Guess he doesn't consider us a threat. Let's go talk to him," Max said, reaching under his seat and grabbing a few things as she climbed out of the truck. A moment later he led the way, arriving at the door a few steps ahead of her.

"What happened to ladies first?" she muttered.

He heard her and smiled. "Navajo habits. We believe the man should lead the way in case there's danger."

"Oh, in that case," she bowed and gestured for him to continue on.

They stepped through the door, ringing an overhead bell, then went up to the counter.

"Good morning," a voice called out from the back. "I'll be right out."

Max and Kris waited by a rack of fishing poles and a moment later the tall Anglo came out to greet them. He was still wearing his pistol, which probably discouraged shoplifting.

"I'm not used to letting in customers early, but it's getting close to hunting season, and with the good weather we've been having, fishermen are taking advantage, too. Name's Harley, but most call me J.D. How can I help you?"

"J.D., we need to ask you a few questions," Max said in an official voice. He pulled back his jacket to show his handgun and extra ammo clips. There was also a set of handcuffs she hadn't noticed before, and a badge she couldn't quite make out except for the word *Navajo*.

Although the hardware was all there, it was Max's cop-like tone that cemented the illusion. Thunder...his code name still rang in her ears. It was tailormade for him.

"Have you seen this man recently, or do you recognize him as a customer?" he asked, showing the proprietor Harris's photo.

"John Harris? Sure. Ex-cop. Recently he's been acquiring a lot of camping equipment. He's decided to catch up on the good life, I guess." He rubbed his chin in contemplation. "He bought a tent, cook stove and some other gear from me. He mentioned that he planned to camp out at some out-of-the-way spot up by Navajo Lake. He was also getting ready for hunting season, Officer..."

"Natoni," Max replied.

He nodded, then continued. "He ended up with a Remington .308 autoloader—no scope." J.D. paused. "But the tribe needs to get together with the other departments on this. Just yesterday afternoon I had this same conversation with another officer…except I forgot to mention that I'd recommended several camping areas to John, all below the quality water at Navajo Lake."

Max said nothing. He simply raised an eyebrow.

The man continued. "But tell me, what's going on? A detective from the Farmington P.D., and now the tribal police?" He glanced at Kris and added, "And which department are you with, ma'am? Your posture tells me you're a cop, too."

"Let's just say I'm not with a local department, J.D.," Kris said, smiling and leaving the conclusions to the proprietor. Thanking him, they bought a good map of the Navajo Dam area, then walked back outside.

"What's bothering you?" she asked as they crossed the parking area.

"After the Farmington police confirmed that the set of dentures on the body belonged to Harris, I was told they'd closed the book and hadn't bothered with DNA testing. But after seeing that officer by Harris's house, and now hearing what J.D. had to say, I'm beginning to think they've got information they're not sharing," Max added.

"Don't assume too much. The officer could have staked out Harris's home, hoping to catch his partner," she pointed out. "It's been clear from the beginning that Harris wasn't working alone."

"Maybe, but the fact that FPD came here to question the sporting goods store owner puts a whole new slant on things. They know at least some of what we know. In fact, they're a step ahead of us," Max stated.

"So what's next? Since we have some idea where he may be camping out and they don't, shall we go to those areas?"

"Yes, but first, let's check out the sporting goods store below Navajo Dam and see if we can narrow down where

Harris is. There are a lot of roads up by the lake, and we'd have to drive for hours otherwise."

They drove most of the way in silence. He would have liked to know what she was thinking right now, but maybe it was better this way. The attraction between them was strong. Too strong. He knew the danger that brought…and the crazy thing was, that instead of making him run for cover, he wanted more of it.

"If we do manage to find him…what then?" she said. "Do we take him down and then call the police, or just alert the police?"

"What would *you* rather do?" Max asked, mostly out of curiosity. He already knew what he intended to do.

She took a deep breath and let it out slowly. "I know what I'd like to do, but I learned something a long time ago—what we want to do most is often what we should not do. In this case, all things considered, I say we keep an eye on him and let the police do the takedown."

He nodded in approval. "We'll only move in if he bolts—of course that's assuming we find him." He thought about the crystal nestled inside his medicine pouch. Eighteen months ago he'd found and saved a Navajo boy's life. A vision in crystal…had it been a dream? He'd certainly never been able to duplicate it, although he'd tried many times since and failed miserably. Despite the fact that others still believed he was a stargazer, he knew better.

"What about your instincts? Cops always say that's what they rely on in a pinch. What do they tell you now?" she asked, cutting into his thoughts.

"To me, what people call instinct is just the product of lessons learned through experience."

"What about woman's intuition? Do you believe in that?" she asked.

There had been no challenge in her voice, only curiosity. He smiled slowly. "Having never experienced it, I can't comment."

She smiled back. "I've learned to rely on mine," she said softly.

Silence stretched out between them again. After several long moments, he spoke. "And what's your intuition telling you about me?"

Kris measured her words carefully. "You define yourself by the work you do and the secrets you keep because, without them, your heart would be too vulnerable," she said, then after a pause, added, "I think you like the barrier that secrets form around you because that's the way you keep other things at bay."

"Other things? Like what?" he asked, curious to know how she saw him.

She hesitated. "People, maybe. Emotions…almost surely."

"Some emotions are…uncertain," he said, shifting uncomfortably. She'd gotten much too close.

"But some emotions can be as certain as the rising of the sun."

"And as misguided as an arrow shot out of a bent quiver."

She smiled. "You've made a home for yourself among secrets. But someday you may find they're not enough."

Max started to answer, then changed his mind. In his gut he knew the truth when he heard it. But she was wrong about one thing. He'd accepted the need to keep the secrets he guarded—especially one. But there was no peace or sense of home inside him because of it. He was a man of facts with a secret that facts didn't support. A stargazer. In his mind he'd seen what he couldn't have possibly known….

"I make a good friend, Max," she said quietly. "And I'm a good keeper of secrets, too." She flashed him a quick smile. "At least the Marine Corps thought so."

He wanted to trust her, to share the details of what had happened. Maybe she could help him make some sense of it all. Kris would make a good friend.

He glanced at her as she leaned back and stretched. Her blouse rode up, revealing the creamy flat expanse of skin below her breasts. The flash of heat that ripped through him took him by surprise.

Who was he kidding? He wanted far more from Kris than just her friendship. But a night of passion with a woman like her could change a man forever.

"We have a job to complete." His voice had come out sounding way too harsh and he knew it the second he glanced over at her. Taking a deep breath, he continued, his voice low. "I want you, Kris. You already know it, you've felt it. But I can't give you what you need."

"You want a one-nighter," she said quietly. "But it wouldn't be like that between us. Don't you sense it?"

He clenched his jaw and nodded, suspecting she was right. But he had nothing to offer her. Until he could make peace with who and what he was—until he came to know himself as either a stargazer or a fraud—he couldn't risk bringing her into his life. What she'd find there might be nothing short of a nightmare. All he could share with her was the present.

"If I could, I'd take you in my arms and show you how we can burn a lifetime of memories into one never-ending night. Neither of us would be the same afterward. But you need more from me than hardness against softness and the pleasures that can bring."

She opened her mouth to speak, but no words came out.

Max saw her hands were trembling, and the way her breath had quickened told him she was fighting herself just as he was.

"You're trouble waiting to happen, Max," she whispered at last, her voice barely audible.

He had no answer to that, so he allowed silence to be his only reply.

SOME TIME LATER they arrived at a sporting goods store located on a side road several miles downstream from Navajo Dam. The terrain was hilly, with steep canyons worn by wind and the more abundant water supply of the higher elevations. Piñon trees covered the slopes.

Kris glanced at Max, then focused back on their surroundings. Their conversation had left her feeling more unsettled than ever. Everything in her longed for a glimpse into the soul of the man beside her. She could feel the loneliness that plagued him and everything in her yearned to reach him, to soothe those feelings away, to help him shoulder his self-imposed burden.

"We're here," Max said at last, interrupting her thoughts.

From where he'd parked, not ten feet from the entrance, they could see inside the store through the tall glass windows. An attached apartment to their left suggested that the owner or a clerk lived on the premises—a good deterrent to break-ins this far from a police station.

"I'm going to try and take Bill, the owner, aside. I've spoken with him a few times before, and I think he'll do his best to help me," Max said.

"It looks like he's got plenty of customers right now, so be careful what you say. We don't want to do or say anything that'll drive his business away."

"You're starting to sound like a kindred shop owner who runs her own business," he said with a quick smile.

"That's what I am," she answered. The nursery was her dream come true. Even though everything else around her had fallen apart, her hopes for it kept her going. The more elusive the dream, the more courage it took to make things happen.

She glanced at Max, so male, so dangerous. He'd be the best…or maybe the worst…of allies. Only time would tell.

Chapter Ten

As they walked inside, two customers were discussing the merits of dry versus wet flies with a young clerk in a baseball-style cap advertising a firearms company. The older man behind the counter put down a mug of coffee and greeted Max like a friend.

"Haven't seen you around here in ages, Max! What have you been up to?"

"Working mostly. I have a job with the tribe these days. Investigations."

"I knew you'd never stop being a cop," he answered with a laugh.

Max introduced Kris to Bill, and then showed him Harris's photo. "Have you seen this man in here?"

He studied the photo, not replying right away. "He looks a bit familiar, but we do a brisk business this time of year. Lots of people taking a late vacation, scouting out hunting grounds or catching up after a busy summer. The rainbows are still biting, especially in the late afternoons and early evenings," he said, still focused on the photo. "I'm not that good with faces, but I'm almost sure I'd remember if he'd bought any rods or reels. He didn't, so if he was here, it was probably just for bait."

Max nodded, his gaze taking in the shop. "Surveillance cameras?" he asked, his voice dropping to a murmur.

Bill nodded. "I had problems with shoplifters. My profit margin couldn't take it, so that's what I did about it. So far it's worked. I keep video for a week before I record over it, if you want to take a look."

"Sure do. Back room?" Max asked.

"You know the way," Bill answered. "The DVDs for the past week are there. Look them over. Just put them back in the order you find them."

"Got it."

Max led Kris into the back room, a combination storage room and employee break area. He'd been in there plenty of times before. Back in the days when he'd been in the force, he'd come fly fishing with his buddies and, sometimes, depending on how the fish were biting, they'd take a break and meet for a few hands of poker.

As he thought back to those days, he felt the sad twinge those memories invariably brought. He'd been a good cop. Then his so-called gift had come into the picture, totally screwing up his career. After the incident with the Navajo boy, even his friends had given him a wide berth. Not that he blamed them. He'd sounded like a loon bucking for the rubber gun squad. In their shoes, he might have done the same.

Pushing those thoughts out of his mind for now, he pulled up a chair and motioned for Kris to do the same. "This may take a while. I'm starting with the most recent surveillance available, then working our way back in time."

Kris went to open the window. "It's stuffy in here. Let's get some air."

When she didn't come back to join him right away, he turned his head and glanced back at her. "Something wrong?"

"No, I just wanted to take a look at the parking lot again. I heard another vehicle pull up. It's a screaming-yellow Jeep. Nothing from the list."

"You remember the makes?" he asked, surprised.

"I have a good memory, but what I was looking for is that

nondescript quality we know Harris would want. A brand new, in-your-face Jeep doesn't fit that bill."

She took a seat beside him, aware of the outdoorsy scent that was so much a part of him. It fit him somehow, emphasizing his independent and untamed spirit.

Kris forced herself to focus on the monitor, unwilling to let herself become distracted now. After several minutes, she leaned back in her chair, her eyes still glued on the screen. Suddenly she sat bolt upright. "There."

He stopped the video and leaned forward.

"Talbot, not Harris," she said, pointing at the image.

"Interesting," Max muttered. "He never struck me as the fishing type."

They continued to watch. Talbot, wearing outdoor clothing and sporting the beginnings of a beard, was paying for items at the counter.

"What's he got?" she asked, leaning forward trying to take a closer look at the purchase.

"Nightcrawlers—worms. They come in those round pint-sized cardboard boxes," he said, pointing. "He must have planned on fishing downstream from the lures—only area below the dam. Hoping for easier, smaller catches."

"The water's different?" she asked.

"No, that's not it. It's usually easier to catch fish with bait than it is with lures. In other words, if you need to eat, you use bait. The purists consider lure fishing, with tied flies and such, more sporting. Since there are fewer fish caught in the lures-only area, the ones there tend to get bigger. Quality water, they call it."

"The readout says he was here yesterday afternoon. Let's check the corresponding parking lot video. Maybe we can connect a vehicle with Talbot," she suggested, reaching for the box labeled Grounds.

"Good thinking," he said, checking the disks and getting the appropriate DVD.

About five minutes later they spotted an older model white pickup with a camper shell. It had no distinctive marks and looked painfully ordinary. A quick check revealed the make and model matched one from the list.

"So they were in this area yesterday," she said, checking the time on the video.

"From what we've seen on the video, they're probably still in the area. Nobody buys bait at the *end* of a fishing trip. We need to check out the camping grounds upstream from here and see if we can spot them." He sighed in frustration. "But this could take a long time. There are over a hundred and fifty miles of shoreline to cover. I've been up here before and some of those roads are tough going."

"Then we better get started," she said.

They headed up the highway, and soon the San Juan River Valley narrowed into a wide canyon flanked by forest-covered mesas on both sides. Every few miles a side road appeared that led down to the river, and they could see vehicles either parked there or moving along dirt tracks that paralleled the shore.

When they were only a few miles from the lures-only water, where the river was shallow and wide to suit fishermen in waders using fly rods, Max turned down a narrow track. They drove on, checking vehicles they passed, waving at the few fishermen who actually turned around to look, but basically striking out.

Talbot and his vehicle were nowhere to be seen.

Soon they reached a wide spot in the river where a fallen log extended out over the deepest channel. There, a sure-footed person could pick their way across grassy, marshy spots to the log, then cross over to the other side of the river and camp among the trees.

Beyond the pines, which came almost up to the bank, they could see a thin plume of gray smoke rising from a campfire. Glimpses of an off-tone green shape visible through the trees suggested a tent had been pitched there.

"Look over there, in the middle of that circle of trees." Kris gestured to a white pickup with a camper shell on their side of the river, parked within a thick grove of pines. "That looks like the one Talbot was using, don't you think?"

"Yeah," he answered with a nod. "Let's disable the truck before we go looking for them. If it's them and they get away from us, they'll have to walk."

"Wait a sec. We can't do that. What if we're wrong, and it belongs to someone else?"

"I'll take away a part that can be easily reinstalled if we're wrong," he said.

He drove past the pickup, then parked about a hundred yards away in a grassy meadow. Max grabbed some hand tools from a box behind the front seat. "Let's go."

Staying low, and circling south to keep from being seen from the opposite shore, they hurried downstream to where the truck was parked. "These older models are easy to open with a slim-jim," Max said, sliding the flat, flexible tool between the glass and the door frame. Within a few seconds he'd opened the lock.

"I don't like this at all, Max. What exactly are you going to do to this truck?"

"I'll remove a battery cable, then hide it somewhere, that's all. If we don't find Harris or Talbot, I'll come back and reinstall it. Satisfied?"

"Okay, but if we come back and the owner is here pitching a fit, you get to do the explaining. Clear?"

He looked up at her and smiled. "Yes, ma'am."

Using the small adjustable wrench he took from his pocket, he loosened the nuts holding one of the battery cables—the ground—then worked it off the terminal. Lastly, he unbolted the other end of the cable from the metal frame.

Kris took the cable from his hand. "I'll handle this part." She walked around to the rear of the truck and placed the cable on the door handle of the entrance to the camper shell. "If we're wrong, it may take the owner a few minutes, but he won't be able to miss it. If this is Talbot's, then we will have still delayed them, so even if they run, we'll be able to catch up to them."

"Okay, get ready to get your feet wet. We may have to do some wading before we reach the log. Once we cross the river, we'll circle around and approach the campsite from the rear." He reached into his pocket and pulled out four self-sealing plastic bags, handing her two.

"For evidence?" she asked.

"No, for anything that has to be protected if we happen to fall in." He placed his cell phone, wallet, keys and medicine pouch in the bags, sealed them up, then returned them to his pockets.

"Let me lead," she said, placing her wallet and the map into one of the bags he'd handed her.

"Why? Don't you think I can handle it?" he asked with a raised eyebrow.

"I'm used to this type of situation, that's all. I just came back from a war zone where there weren't any well-defined front lines. We had to use extreme caution even when approaching things that looked perfectly innocent. This past year-and-a-half I've spent my waking hours looking for trip wires, buried explosives, and land mines before taking the next step." She met his eyes. "You have a tendency to go with your gut, like when you rushed the guys at the cemetery, but my training can give us the edge now."

He nodded and waved her on. "Ladies first, then."

They managed to pick their way through the marsh, which was nearly dry this time of year, without even getting their pants wet. Then they reached the log. Alert for slippery spots, she led the way across it at a brisk pace. Her sense of balance had always been excellent.

"Keep in mind that a sniper's a possibility, too," she whispered, looking into the brush and trees beyond for activity.

"The men we're hunting are nothing if not cautious, and they have at least one rifle."

"I don't think they'd risk a shot unless we cornered them. It would draw too much attention, and everyone has a cell phone nowadays. They'll be more likely to bolt—which is why I wanted to disable the truck."

The mashed-down footprints in the grass leading away from the river left a clear path, one that they were reluctant to follow, leery of a trap.

They walked upstream instead, remaining as close as they could to the river's narrow bank and using the sound of the rushing water to mask the sound of their footsteps. The lower terrain also concealed them from view. About a hundred yards upstream from the trail, they headed away from the river, angling in the direction of the campsite. Although the trees gave them plenty of cover, it also obscured their line of sight, and they had to feel their way forward.

"I don't see the smoke any more. Maybe we're still too close to the river," Max whispered, then started to go around her.

"Stop," she said harshly.

"What do you see?" he asked.

"Check out the bootprints." She pointed to their right. "They look like the ones we saw in Harris's house. One shoe has the same slice across the heel."

"Harris is—or was—here, then. But we need to make sure before we call it in."

"Judging from these tracks, he circled his own camp-ground, too," she warned. "Stay sharp. He may have left a surprise or two for unexpected visitors."

"No way they'd risk an explosive or booby trap here," Max answered, looking around. "Fishermen working their way up or downstream constantly wander through each other's campsites. Killing one of them would get a busload of officers out here."

They made their way slowly through the thick undergrowth and around the pine trees, staying low and communicating only through hand gestures. The scent of a campfire drifted past them first, then they heard indistinct voices ahead, about forty yards or so.

Kris caught a sudden flash of light on the ground before her. Realizing that Max was about to take a step, she reached over and yanked him back hard. They both tumbled to the grass and rolled into a low stop.

Max ended up on top of her, his eyes gleaming with desire. For a heartbeat, as the hardness of his body pressed intimately against her, she forgot to breathe.

"I'm all for this, you know, but it'll have to wait," he murmured. He stared into her eyes for one long moment as if memorizing each and every sensation, then rolled away and sat up, looking around to make sure they hadn't alarmed their prey.

She struggled to clear her thoughts. "Trip wire," she whispered, rising to a crouch.

She followed the length of nylon line, placed about six inches above the ground, and running between two low branches of adjacent pines. Hanging beneath one of the pines, a foot off the ground, were two tin cans. They probably had some pebbles inside them. Moving the trip wire would have rattled the cans—an old warning device that Harris or Talbot couldn't have missed.

"Early warning signal," she whispered, then continued.

Finding an open area that was too risky to cross, they were forced to head closer to the river, back alongside the bank where they'd come upstream not ten minutes earlier. The footing was precarious there, but again, the water masked the sounds of their footsteps and the embankment gave them cover.

They listened carefully for the voices ahead, and although from their vantage point, they couldn't make out what the men were saying, they were a lot closer now.

Max signaled Kris, then moved up the embankment, crouching low to reduce his silhouette, more careful where he stepped now. As they drew closer, he caught a glimpse of the green tent through the trees. Harris was on his knees, shifting the coals of a campfire with a stick. A coffeepot was above the fire on a metal grill.

As Max turned to signal Kris, his movement spooked several young ducks swimming downstream. The entire flock took flight, quacking and flapping wildly.

The next instant a shot rang out and the bullet ricocheted off a rock just beside him, whining off into the distance. He turned in a crouch and, grabbing Kris's hand, dove into the river just as several more bullets followed.

They swam downstream, beneath the icy cold river as long as they could, then surfaced, gasping for air. Sixty yards away, and well past the log, they made their way quickly to the shore. They covered each other, weapons in hand, as they slowly made their way back upstream. When they reached the log, they saw fresh footprints in the mud and crossed as quickly as possible to the other bank.

"Hurry. We need to get to the trees," Kris said as they ran through the marsh, retracing their previous route.

They reached solid ground at an old embankment where the river used to flow, and as they were scrambling up, they heard a vehicle racing away. A rising cloud of dust farther up the road led toward the highway.

Max cursed. "All because of those blasted ducks!"

"They must have had a second car nearby," she said, coming up to stand beside him.

"Let's get to the truck and see if we can pick up their trail," Max said, walking briskly forward.

Kris fell into step beside him, pushing her jacket back and pulling her knit top away from her body.

"You'd win the wet T-shirt contest," he said, his eyes searing over her at the same time he maintained his stride.

Her gaze drifted over his cotton shirt, still pasted to his chest. "No, actually, you would."

He gave her an infinitely masculine grin. "Another time, another place, we'll continue this discussion."

They both picked up the pace at the same time, breaking into a jog as they headed upstream to where he'd parked his truck.

"You really *do* look amazing," he said, stealing another quick look at her.

Her skin prickled as his gaze caressed her breasts. He didn't even have to touch her to make her senses spring to life. She'd always dreamed of a man who could make her feel this way, but this wasn't their time, not with bullets likely to come flying at them at any given moment.

Yet the same ever-present danger that heightened her senses also made her acutely aware of everything about him— the heat from his body, the way his dark eyes seemed to light up with an inner fire whenever he looked at her.

"Focus," she said, mostly to herself.

"Don't worry. Harris isn't getting away," he answered, unaware.

They reached his truck a few minutes later, but it was soon obvious they weren't going anywhere. Two tires were flat. Max spat out a vicious oath. "He did it to me again. I have one spare, not two."

"Then let's take Talbot's wheels," she said gesturing toward the trees where the white pickup was hidden. "We know where his battery cable is, and I'm sure you know how to hot-wire an older model like that."

They jogged to the nondescript two-door truck with the camper shell, then quickly reattached the battery cable. Max jumped into the driver's seat and looked down at the ignition. "Crap, he cut pieces out of the wiring."

"He couldn't drive it, so neither could we. But we need transportation from somewhere," Kris said.

"We could wait an hour or so for help, or…" He glanced

at another truck parked about fifty yards farther upstream. "It's got a Navajo tribal agency bumper sticker. See it?"

"So we find the owner and ask him for his keys. You have lots of tribal connections, so that should help."

Max looked around, but no one was in sight. "He might have hiked on up to the quality water. We can't take time to search for the guy, and if he's waded out into the stream, we can't exactly get to him without waders. Harris is making tracks as we speak."

"So what do you propose?" she asked in a guarded tone.

"Some tribal employees keep a spare key hidden somewhere in case they lock themselves out. Start checking under the fenders for a magnetic holder."

Max found what he was searching for in the left rear tire well, the second place he looked. "Here it is. We lucked out."

Kris slipped into the passenger's side and opened the glove compartment. Finding a small notepad and pencil, she started to write. "One minute."

"What are you doing?"

"We're going to leave a note on that tree right next to where he parked. He's bound to see it," she said, then showed him what she's written.

It read, "'Tribal Emergency. Special Investigator Natoni, Office of Tribal President. Call to verify. Your vehicle will be returned later today.'"

"Fine. Don't waste time trying to pin it to the tree. Leave it on the ground with a rock on top. We have to get going right now."

Instead of doing as he asked, she impaled it on a small branch at eye level.

"Okay, now I'm ready," she said, jumping back into the passenger's side.

"We've wasted too much time. Hang on to something. I'm going to make a fast exit," he said, then raced back down the dirt track. He picked up even more speed as they hit the paved road, turning east.

▶ If offer card is missing write to: Harlequin Reader Service, 3010 Walden Ave., P.O. Box 1867, Buffalo, NY 14240-1867 ▶

NO POSTAGE
NECESSARY
IF MAILED
IN THE
UNITED STATES

BUSINESS REPLY MAIL
FIRST-CLASS MAIL   PERMIT NO. 717   BUFFALO NY

POSTAGE WILL BE PAID BY ADDRESSEE

HARLEQUIN READER SERVICE
3010 WALDEN AVE
PO BOX 1867
BUFFALO NY 14240-9952

Send For
2 FREE BOOKS
Today!

I accept your offer!

Please send me two free *Harlequin Intrigue*® novels and two mystery gifts (gifts worth about $10). I understand that these books are completely free—even the shipping and handling will be paid—and I am under no obligation to purchase anything, ever, as explained on the back of this card.

382 HDL ERR7   **182 HDL ERVW**

Please Print

FIRST NAME

LAST NAME

ADDRESS

APT.#   CITY

STATE/PROV.   ZIP/POSTAL CODE

Offer limited to one per household and not valid to current subscribers of *Harlequin Intrigue*® books.

"What made you decide to head toward the lake? They had to have left all, or most, of their camping gear behind when they took off," she said.

"John's smart. He'd know we'd think of that and use it against us. Instead of doing what we would expect him to do, head back to a community, he'll go in exactly the opposite direction."

Kris brought out the map of the lake area from the plastic bag that had kept it dry. "There's a turnoff not too many miles ahead, south on Highway 539. What if he plans to take that route, circle around, then come up behind *us* on the way back to civilization? The hunted would all of a sudden become the hunter again."

"Now you're thinking like a cop. So we take Highway 539, keep our eyes open and hope to get behind him instead."

Max pressed down on the accelerator, and within fifteen minutes, they were heading south.

"The bad part is that we don't even know what kind of car or truck we're looking for anymore," she said, noting that her clothes were almost dry now. "Our chances of finding them are slim."

"Considering the primitive roads in this area, it'll be a truck or an SUV. There'll be two men inside. Search for that."

She nodded. Although she was trying not to get discouraged, she couldn't quite push back the feeling that she'd somehow failed Tina. Her eyes filled with tears, and she forced herself not to blink, determined not to let him see her crying.

Although Max had been concentrating on the road, he'd somehow sensed her change of mood. Reaching over, he covered her hand with his own. "We'll find them again. Trust me on that."

She was about to answer when they heard the wail of a siren behind them. In the rearview mirrors, they could see a police car, closing in fast.

Chapter Eleven

She'd hoped that the white police cruiser would just pass them by, but as the sheriff's department car pulled up behind them with lights flashing, she knew they were in big trouble.

"Maybe the owner of this truck didn't buy the note. Or maybe he didn't see it," Max said slowly.

"So we're about to be arrested for grand theft auto?" Her voice rose an octave.

"I'll handle it," he said firmly. "Sit tight and let me do all the talking. And keep your Beretta under the seat."

When the officer came over to the driver's side window, Max relaxed. "Hey, Robert," he said, giving the deputy a nod. He also knew this man, a member of the Brotherhood, as Guardian.

Deputy Robert Joe, a Navajo, served with the county sheriff's department. He came closer, glanced inside the cab of the truck, nodded to Kris, then turned back to Max. "What's the deal here? You know you're driving a stolen truck."

It hadn't been a question. "Borrowed—that is, unless the person who drove it before me had it illegally," Max corrected. "I had a tribal emergency, and this is a tribal vehicle. I'm empowered. A note was left at the scene."

Deputy Joe shook his head. "If we were on the Rez, it would be different, but here, I answer to another authority. I'm going to have to take your guns—I'm assuming you're both armed—and bring you in. But we'll dispense with the cuffs. Just follow me in. I'm sure we can clear it up fast."

Max looked at the road ahead. Harris was long gone, regardless of the direction. Rather than risk exposing the identity of another member of the Brotherhood by asking to be released on his own recognizance, he decided to go along with it.

"Okay," he said at last, handing over his weapon, and signaling Kris to do the same. "We'll come in and get this straightened out."

"Where are your wheels?" Joe asked.

"Last turnoff before the quality water begins. The blue pickup with two punctured tires." Max added the license number and make.

"I'll have a safety aide go get it."

"There's a spare in the wheel well," Max answered.

They followed the police cruiser west toward the Blanco substation. It wasn't until they were well on their way that Kris finally spoke.

"That went down too easy. He never asked for your name, or mine. You two know each other…but it goes beyond that, doesn't it?"

"Yes, it does."

"And it's more than both of you being part of the same tribe, or you being an ex-cop." When he didn't answer right away, she looked at him. "You're putting off the inevitable, you know. You can't keep a secret like this from someone whose neck is on the line right alongside yours. One of these times you're going to need something from me that'll require complete trust between us."

Max still remained silent.

"All right, have it your way," she said with a sigh. "But here's what I've put together on my own. You're part of something that's symbolized by that carving on the safe house door. It's an organization of some sort and it may—or may not—have anything to do with the tribal president. Despite that, the organization is important enough to have serious clout—the kind that can get us both out of fixes like these."

He looked at her, surprised. "That's quite an interesting dossier you've got for me—everything but a date of birth."

"I'll honor your need to keep your ties to that organization a secret. Don't worry about that."

No wonder she'd gotten under his skin. Kris had it all—a body to die for, brains, and character. And even more important…she knew about discretion. The fact that she intended to keep a secret that wasn't hers told him that she was the kind of woman a man like him would be proud to have by his side. But what had blown him completely away was that she hadn't used what she'd put together as a springboard to get the rest of the story.

"You never cease to amaze me," he said at last. "You're one helluva woman."

She smiled. "You're finally catching on."

He was still smiling as they pulled into the station, a small office flanked on either side by a barbershop and a feed store in the small community of Blanco. Joe came over and met them as they got out of the car.

"Your truck is being towed in, and the tribe will foot the bill. Come on inside. With luck, this won't take long."

Max and Kris had to make separate statements, but once those were checked to make sure there were no discrepancies, they were free to go. The Navajo driver of the tribal truck had decided not to press charges. He'd apologized, in fact, for his mistake, claiming not to have seen the note before reporting the theft. Apparently he'd seen Max driving off and had been too upset at the time to notice anything else.

Max and Kris were at the desk ready to pick up their weapons when Deputy Joe came back. "I've told them that you have a permit to carry concealed, and that's been verified along with the appropriate serial numbers. But it turns out there was another weapon just lying in the bed of your truck. That doesn't sound like you. You're never careless. So what's the deal?"

Max recalled Jerry's pistol, but he'd ditched it already. "You saw our weapons, and there weren't supposed to be any others in my vehicle—none belonging to me or Ms. Reynolds, anyway. Let me take a look at the gun you found."

Joe led the way to an office down the hall, then opened the locked file. He extracted a handgun with an attached tag and held it by the trigger guard.

Max gave the weapon a long, careful look. "I always use the Beretta, or a Browning High Power, both in 9 mm. That's a .380 Sig P232." He thought about it a moment. "A few plainclothes officers prefer that make and model. Considering who we've been around lately, I think that may be Harris's gun—the one he used to shoot me and Tina Reynolds."

He heard Kris suck in her breath, but when he turned to look at her, there was no trace of emotion on her face.

Deputy Joe brought out an evidence pouch, put the pistol inside, then started to label the contents.

Another deputy came in just then, interrupting the process. "I'm here," he said, sitting behind one of the desks. "Just read me the serial numbers and I'll run them through the system right now."

It took about five minutes for the verifications to take place. The gun was confirmed to be one that had been reported stolen from the Farmington Police Department's evidence room a few years ago—while John Harris was still a member of the force. Max's statement, from a few days ago, served to verify that Harris had used a weapon of that make and model in the shootings.

Kris was soon taken to one interrogation room while Max was brought into another. His escort was a potbellied sergeant named Garson with breath that was three-quarters green chile and one-quarter stale coffee.

"How did this pistol get in your truck?" Garson asked him

pointedly. "If this weapon matches the one used to kill Tina Reynolds Greer, it links you to that shooting."

"If it turns out to be the same one that killed my companion that day, it's also the one used to shoot me. Why would I withhold any evidence under those circumstances?"

"So explain how it got in the bed of your truck."

"My companion and I left my pickup and went on foot to track down a suspect we believed to be camping in that area," he said, avoiding mentioning Harris. "When we came back, someone had flattened two of my truck's tires. That's when I commandeered a tribal vehicle. My truck was left sitting there by the river for over two hours. Anyone could have placed the pistol in there during that time."

"Who do you think did that, and why?" Garson demanded.

"Bruce Talbot. I believe he was John Harris's accomplice during the attempted robbery that resulted in my partner's death," Max answered.

Telling the sergeant that he suspected Harris was still alive would almost guarantee that they wouldn't leave the station for hours. This was the quickest way.

"I followed a lead that placed Talbot in that area using a particular vehicle, so we went to look for him. We found the vehicle—it's listed in the report—but we never saw Talbot. When we returned to my truck, we saw the two flats." He held Garson's gaze. "Think about this. If I'd found the gun that was used to shoot me and kill my partner, why would I jeopardize critical evidence by throwing it in the back of my pickup, and why would I hang on to it in the first place? It makes no sense that I'd be so careless with evidence that could be used to convict my assailant."

"So you think it was Talbot...but why would he plant it there? He had no idea you'd end up at the station and that we'd be towing in your truck."

Max considered it for several moments. "How many calls did you get on the tribal truck?" he asked.

The light of recognition flickered in the officer's steady gaze. "I'll check on that," he said and left the room. It took him several minutes, but when he returned, he didn't seem so ready to leap for Max's jugular. "Two—the tribal guy and someone else, who didn't give his name. The unidentified guy said he was calling for the victim of the theft. His was actually the first call, and the cell phone he used was a throwaway so it can't be traced to an owner, just the purchase site."

"Talbot," Max answered. "He wanted to hold me up here long enough to make a clean getaway."

"Why is he running from you?"

"Because he's connected to the crimes I'm investigating," Max answered flatly.

Garson continued to press for more information, but without more evidence—all he had was a gun that belonged to a man the police ostensibly believed to be dead—he couldn't hold them. It took another twenty minutes before they were finally allowed to leave, with the usual warning about not leaving the county.

"I didn't think they'd ever let us go," Kris said as they hit the road.

"They had to. I obviously didn't shoot myself. The shots were fired from a distance beyond the reach of my arm, and the angle of the bullet wounds made that impossible anyway. Of course my prints weren't on the gun, and neither were yours. No prints at all were found, in fact. Basically they didn't have enough to keep us."

"I bet your tribal friends also exerted some pull," she remarked.

"Probably," he conceded, then glanced around. "We've lost critical time—which I'm convinced is the reason that gun was planted in my truck. We probably won't be able to pick up Harris and Talbot's trail now."

"But we have to try," she said, finishing his unspoken thought.

"Yes, we do. That's why I'm going back to Navajo Dam.

We'll talk to any fishermen we can find in the area, and also check out Talbot and Harris's campsite. Let's see what kinds of leads we can get."

They'd only driven east for about four minutes when he suddenly slowed and turned down a dirt road leading southeast, paralleling a wide arroyo.

"What's going on? We pick up some company?" Kris asked, checking in the passenger side mirror.

"Looks like it. The same old Jeep has been following us since we left the station. Though he's staying well back, he's there. If he makes the same turn, it won't be coincidental."

"Who do you think it is? Someone from the Sheriff's Department?"

"I don't think so. At first I thought Harris had planted the gun on us so we'd be held up at the station—a delaying tactic, you know? But maybe I missed the real reason for it. Maybe it was his way of giving himself time to pick us up again, once we were released, that is. He's probably come to the conclusion that we're worth more to him running around loose than tied up in the back of his van—that is *if* he can tail us."

"Are you sure he took the turn with us? We're going down Cañon Largo, but I don't see anyone following." There was no rising cloud of dust behind them, nor were there any vehicles in the area.

"He's there. Look in the arroyo to our right. He wasn't about to follow us down this road because he knew he'd give himself away."

She watched for a while, then finally nodded. "I just saw a flash of green. He's in there."

"If he stays there a little longer, we've got him. I've been in this area lots of times—Gobernador is near one of the tribe's four sacred mountains, see it over there?" He pointed to his left.

From the distance, it looked like any other sandstone mesa—steeper on one side, more or less rounded off elsewhere, and dotted with juniper and piñon pines. But it had special significance to the tribe, and even non-Navajos treated it with upmost respect. "Gobernador Knob. What do the Navajos call it?"

"Gobernador Knob."

She rolled her eyes.

"Okay. The *Diné* also call it *Ch'óol'í'í*. It's said to be clothed in sacred jewels. First Man and First Woman found a baby on top, and the girl grew up to be Changing Woman, mother of the Hero Twins. They were the ones who cleared the land of monsters."

"Speaking of monsters," she said, glancing behind them. "How do we get rid of Harris and Talbot?"

"You're about to find out. Hang on!"

Max suddenly swerved to the right, heading down a fork in the road that led them south, toward the arroyo where Harris was driving.

Realizing that they were on to him, Harris turned hard and took the right fork in the arroyo, racing away from them.

Max continued farther down the fork, then came upon a muddy stream blocking their path. He slowed, put the pickup into four-wheel drive, then inched slowly across the water to the far side, a distance of about twenty feet.

"Easy ford. That was less than two feet deep. Harris will have to cross it, too, though he's farther south, right?"

Max snorted. "I hope he tries. This channel, which connects with Navajo Lake, is called Cutter Canyon. When it's two feet deep here, it's three feet deeper farther downstream, especially where it enters that arroyo." He paused. "Even if he makes it across, he'll end up going in the wrong direction after about a mile. The only way for him to get back on our trail is by going all the way back to the highway."

The area, part of the San Juan Basin Gas Field, was covered with natural gas wells and access roads, and he skillfully led them back to the highway, halfway between their original

turn-off point and the small collection of homes and busi-
nesses optimistically named Navajo City.

Confident that they'd lost Harris—at least for now—Max
pulled over to the side of the highway.

"What's up?" she asked quickly. He'd impressed her with
his inventiveness in losing Harris. When it came to matters
pertaining to the Four Corners area, he was supremely confident, and that added to her confidence in him.

As she studied the way his strong hands gripped the wheel,
her mind wandered. For a minute she imagined them on her
bare skin, touching and caressing her.

"Hello?"

Surprised, she looked at him quickly. "I'm sorry. Did you
say something?"

"You had the most peculiar expression on your face," he
added. "Stay focused."

"I am focused," she said, not clarifying what she'd been
focused on.

He grinned as if he'd read her mind.

"So what next?" she asked, wanting to divert him.

"If I can get a signal, I'm going to use the cell phone and
get in touch with a friend. He's helped us before."

"Another member of your group," she guessed.

He didn't answer, no longer surprised by how quickly she
filled in the blanks. He flipped open his cell phone. "No
signal. I'll have to park and walk a little farther up that rise,"
he said, pointing with his lips, Navajo style. "Maybe I can get
something from there."

"All right. I'll keep watch, just in case."

Moments later, Max parked. As he strode away, she
watched him. He came alive when courting danger—the very
thing she'd hoped to avoid once she returned stateside.

Yet a man like Max was a warrior for life and needed
things that were vastly different from the peaceful lifestyle she
craved. Secrets would always be a part of him and his world,

too, and along with those secrets came danger and uncertainty. But no one had ever made her feel like he did. Max was at the heart of all the fantasies she'd indulged in most of her life.

She brought her thoughts back to the danger at hand as she saw a truck coming down the road from the west. Seconds later, seeing it was just teens out for a drive, she breathed a sigh of relief. By then, Max had returned.

"We need to lay low for a bit. There's an old abandoned trading post just a few miles up this road. We can hide out there until my friend can bring us a new set of wheels."

"Is something wrong with your truck?" she asked quickly as he climbed back inside and started the engine.

"Not specifically, but Harris will recognize it in a flash no matter where we go. Also, somebody I don't know worked on this truck. If Harris has contacts in this area, or if he set us up even more than we realize, we could be carrying a hidden GPS tracking device. Switching cars is the simplest and safest solution."

She agreed, but didn't reply as they drove east, toward a steep canyon bordered by two mesas. There was greater elevation there, and the junipers were thick.

Minutes stretched out and when she still hadn't said anything, he glanced over at her. "You're too quiet all of a sudden."

"I'm trying to figure out how we can turn this game of cat-and-mouse around and get the upper hand. The key is finding the platinum, of course, but the truth is I have no idea what my sister meant by 'remember.'"

"Neither do I," he admitted. "I'm hoping that as we close in on what she did that day, one of us will be able to figure out the answer. I've searched my memory for days, wondering if she meant for me to remember something she'd said just before Harris turned on us, but nothing makes sense. Up to that moment, it was just another job."

Before long, just beyond the narrow pass between the two mesas, they turned south onto a well service road. They made several turns in that direction, and eventually pulled into the former parking lot of a trading post. The door was half-open, a tumbleweed blocking the way. The roof of the long, narrow veranda had been damaged by the wind. Pieces of the corrugated metal were curled up like corn chips. The building, up close, didn't seem that old, and it became clear that the log walls had been weathered and distressed to make the building seem more frontierlike. Then she saw the massive hole that had been punched through the north wall.

"What happened to this place?" she asked.

"An Anglo man died here a few years ago. This is mostly a traditionalist area, so a hole was punched into the wall to let out his *chindi* and to warn others that a death had occurred here. Not many Navajos will dare visit this place now."

"So why did *you* choose this as a meeting place? You're Navajo, but Harris isn't."

"Harris was a Farmington cop taught to know some of the basic Navajo customs and practices. He won't be expecting me to come here. And even if he has a GPS hidden on the truck, he'll still have to circle around and find the right road."

"Good thinking."

They'd only been there a few minutes when she called Max's attention to a primer-gray SUV coming their way.

"I see it. Hang tight." Max picked up his cell phone and spoke a few quick words in Navajo. "Okay, you can relax," he told Kris a second later. "It's my friend."

Max turned off the engine—something he hadn't done until now just in case they'd been forced to take off fast. "I'll go talk to him. Give me a moment."

"No problem," she said, although the truth was she had no intention of doing as he asked. She wanted to know everything about Max Natoni and to do that she'd have to start breaking a few rules. Now was as good a time as any to start. She reached for the door handle.

Chapter Twelve

Max approached his cousin, Wind, and gave him a nod in greeting. "Nice set of wheels," he said, looking at the Jeep. "Not so pretty, but invisible at night. Any extras?"

"Something you can use—run-flat tires. Then there's the usual goodies…auxiliary fuel tank, fuel injected V-8 and a stability and handling package. It'll beat any SUV on the road, and off-road as well. It's also got two tracking devices—one's easy to find in case the perps get their hands on these wheels. The other's hidden so we can still keep an eye on this vehicle's location. It's there mostly to help us keep tabs on you. We'll be around in case you need help."

"Good, I hope that won't be necessary, but it's appreciated."

"I've also got a message for you from *Hastiin Bigodii*," Wind said, pausing to glance at Kris, who'd stepped out of the truck and was walking around.

Thunder followed his gaze, then nodded back to him. "It's okay. Go on."

Before Wind could answer, Kris called out to him. "I'm going to stretch my legs for a bit. Any objections?"

"Go ahead," Max answered. "I'll be done in a few minutes." He then turned his attention back to Wind. "Okay, continue."

"We checked out the gas station the old man went to after finding your partner's body, and were able to interview the attendant who was there that day. He remembers some of the details, but rather than hear the story from me, I think you'll understand more if you get the particulars from him directly. You'll want to ask your own questions, too."

"Where do I go, and who do I need to see?" Max asked.

"The place is on the south side of Highway 64, just past Red Wash and a few miles east of Beclabito."

"Not too far from where the incident went down," he said, then added, "That's a traditionalist area, too, right?"

Wind nodded. "The attendant goes by the name of *Cháala Nééz*, tall Charlie. And the station doesn't close until six, so you've got plenty of time."

Max looked at his watch. It was a good hour-and-a-half drive, with Beclabito just a few miles on the New Mexico side of the Arizona border. "I'll go have a talk with him," he affirmed.

"*Hastiin Bigodii* wanted to know if you've tried to use your gift again. If you haven't, he asked that you keep trying."

"That's…difficult."

"To accept the gift as yours, or to try when you've got company with you?"

"Both."

"I don't think you give the woman enough credit," Wind said with a ghost of a smile. "She's smart and resourceful, though not as quiet as she'd hope to be. My guess is your ability wouldn't phase her much."

Knowing Wind wasn't the type to make a statement like that without basis, Max gave him a hard look. "And just how would you know she's smart and resourceful—and not so quiet?"

"She apparently circled us when we weren't looking," he said, now speaking in a whisper. "No telling how much of our conversation she actually heard."

Max turned his head and saw a shape just beyond the trees walking hurriedly back toward the pickup. "I'll handle this," he told Wind, handing him the keys to the pickup.

"Good luck," Wind said, giving him the Jeep's keys, then

walked off toward Max's truck. A minute later, he drove off, nodding to Kris, who'd just come out of the forest.

While Max checked the SUV, Kris walked over, then climbed into the passenger's side. "We have a very good lead," he said, "But of course you know that already."

"How would I know that?" she countered.

"You went around us and overheard what we said." He started the engine and turned down a road he knew would lead him back to the main highway. He planned to head west toward Shiprock and beyond.

"If you knew I was there, then you must have wanted me to know," she responded without hesitation.

He wasn't about to admit that Wind had been the one to hear her footsteps, so he remained silent.

"Tell me about your gift," she asked softly.

He shook his head. "It's nearly impossible to explain. It's something that's rooted in the beliefs of my tribe."

"And you don't think I could understand?" she asked, sounding hurt. "I grew up within sight of Ship Rock—the formation, not the town—and a lot of my classmates were Navajo. Give me a little credit."

Max rubbed the back of his neck with one hand. "It's not something I'd normally talk about with someone who's not Navajo. I'm not even sure I understand it. I work with facts. I'm comfortable with them. But this—it defies any rational explanation."

"*Not* talking about it won't make it go away," she insisted.

"No, it won't, but it's one way of not having to think about it. I've put it out of my mind, and I suggest you do the same."

His tone precluded any further discussion, and he was glad when she took the hint. He glanced down at the *jish* on his belt, which had been sealed in one of the plastic bags, and fortunately wasn't damaged by the dip in the river. Gazing at the crystal he carried in there now had accomplished the impossible once before, but he'd never been able to do it again, not even to locate the platinum that had claimed the life of his friend. *Hastiin Bigodii* didn't understand the concept of a fluke—a one-shot event—but he strongly suspected that was all his so-called gift had been.

As he drove down the road, he told her about the gas station attendant and where they were headed. To his own surprise, she asked him no questions and didn't even comment. Her silence puzzled him, and he wondered if it was because they were heading into the area where Tina had lost her life. Or maybe Kris was just exhausted. He gave her a quick sideways glance.

Kris was leaning back, her eyes closed. Her shirt had worked open at the collar, revealing a round, creamy breast encased in a pink lacy bra. Her softness whispered to him, tempting him. Man required woman. Only by pairing could either be complete. Harmony and beauty required balance…and unity.

Everything male in him longed to make her his. He was aware of Kris in ways that defied logic. At the same time it infuriated him that the merest glimpse of her breast could heat his blood like this. He took a breath. Distractions in a case like this one could prove fatal—but she was much more than a distraction and he knew it.

"Do you think Talbot is Harris's only partner?" she asked at last, shifting and opening her eyes.

"I think so, but I don't know for sure. That's why we have to stay sharp and on our guard."

An hour later, west of Rattlesnake and deep into the juniper, piñon forest around Beclabito, he pulled into an ancient gasoline station. The building dated back to the 1950s, but one of the bays now contained soda, chips, candy and a few basics, such as milk and bread. The pumps had been updated, and all but three of the four were now self-serve.

"Let's gas up first, then we'll go talk to the attendant," Max said.

After filling up, they went inside to pay. The young clerk

behind the counter looked about twenty and was answering the phone when Max came up to the counter.

Max reached for his wallet and glanced around, making sure no other customers were in the building. "*Cháala Nééz?*" he asked.

The young man nodded.

"I need to talk to you about the old man who reported the murdered Anglo woman's body," he said softly, knowing that talk of death was often believed capable of attracting the dead.

"I was told you'd be by, uncle," the attendant said, using the term out of respect, not to denote kinship. "The man you're looking for called from that phone." He indicated a phone at the far end of the counter. "He was really scared, too. He'd been out gathering firewood when lightning struck a tree close to where he'd been standing. That spooked him, and then he found the woman's car, with blood all over the seats and stuff. A short distance from there he saw her body."

"Go on," Max urged when the man grew silent for a moment.

"He said he drove like crazy after that. He stopped only to buy some canned meat and other food for the drive to Arizona. He wanted to find a *hataalii* who could help him. I convinced him to make that call to the police before he left because it was the law—reporting crimes and stuff. Gets him off the hook, you know."

"Did you recommend a *hataalii?*" Max asked, knowing they could track down the medicine man.

The young man shook his head. "I didn't know one, not around here. I go to the public health clinic when I get sick."

"Do you know the old man's name?" Max pressed.

He shook his head. "He never gave me one. Traditionalists don't like to use names, you know. All I can tell you is that he's not from around here. He might be from that outfit—" he said, using the word that on the Rez meant a group of relatives who work cooperatively "—that lives up by Hidden Valley, west of Toadlena. Several of the families make money gathering firewood, then selling it by the road near Window Rock during the tribal fair."

Trying to get more specific directions to where the Navajos went to gather firewood, and ruling out most of the area close to Shiprock, took a while longer. Almost a quarter of New Mexico was forest land, but the forests were scattered among several small ranges. The most likely locations were in the foothills and mountain slopes along the Arizona border.

The young man ended up calling his dad, and together they came up with a list.

Once they were on their way, Max filled her in. "We'll be going back through Shiprock, then south toward Gallup. When we reach the road to Toadlena, we'll head toward the mountains. Hidden Valley is beyond the community of Toadlena, among the foothills of the Chuska Mountains. It's in the piñon juniper foothills. We should get there about four o'clock."

"What do you think our chances are of finding this man?" she asked.

"It'll depend on whether we can get anyone at all to talk to us. That's going to be tricky, so be prepared. We can't just walk up to someone's house and knock. We have to wait to be invited to approach. And they may decide never to invite us if they don't like the way we look for some reason." After noting her cocked eyebrow, he explained. "Our traditionalists have their own way of doing things, and they don't like visitors after dark, if it ends up taking us that long to get there. Night is always considered a dangerous time."

"Is there anything in particular I should avoid doing or saying?"

"Whatever you do, *never* speak of the dead. Also, remember that words have power and speaking about something can bring it into existence. So be very careful what you say." He paused, then continued. "Does that all seem really strange to you?"

"People all over the world have different ways of going

about their lives. In the Middle East, where I spent most of the past two years, everything seemed strange to me at first. Then I came to the realization that beyond skin tones, beyond the shape of the eyes, lies another human being and that's what ties us together."

He smiled at her. "Navajos believe that all things are interconnected. What you've just said isn't far from our own beliefs."

"Respect is the key. By honoring the differences between us, I can walk in beauty, too," she said softly.

Her words wound through him and touched a piece of his soul. By bringing Kris into his life, fate had given him a gift. Now the choice was his—reach out to her, or let her slip away. But he had no clear answers beyond that.

They stopped at a fast-food place in Shiprock just long enough to pick up a late lunch, then ate along the way. After turning off the busy main highway, the notoriously danger-ous road previously listed as Highway 666, the drive to Toadlena was quiet and peaceful.

Sheep and goats grazed aimlessly beneath the afternoon sky, or gathered in flocks guarded by watchful dogs and Navajos on horseback. Windmills and stock tanks spoke about the Navajo way of life better than words could express.

"I grew up just outside Shiprock, and I swore I'd never live out here with these hicks," he said with a quirky half smile as they passed through the small village of Toadlena. "But it doesn't look half-bad to me now."

"I can't even imagine what it would be like to live out here, say at that house," she said, pointing straight ahead to a simple square house kept company by a small corral, a pickup truck and several large water tanks. "His closest neighbor is just a single point of light off in the distance," she added, gesturing to the right.

"That's exactly why they've chosen to live out here. Their relatives may not live close by, but they're always there when needed. People on the outside of our borders often live in crowded cities or towns but barely know the people next door."

"How do they deal with the isolation?" she asked quietly.

"They join clubs or churches so they can find connections with others who share their beliefs and preferences. No matter what, a Navajo is always part of the tribe, and never alone." He paused for a moment, deep in thought. "On the outside, people worry about things like bad luck and illness. We're taught ways to handle all those things. We have Good Luck songs, we have ceremonies—but most of all, we have each other."

"I envy you that. The busy world of the average Anglo is based on totally different values. All that counts is the individual and his drive to succeed. Competition, and particularly coming out number one, is everything."

"Here we learn a different way."

"Yes, one where inner peace can become more than just words," she answered.

He nodded. "That's why you and I have to restore the *hózhg,* the harmony and balance, and to do that, we have to find the elderly man who discovered your sister's body. He's out here somewhere."

"We're past Toadlena now so I guess it's time to get to work," she said.

Max nodded.

They drove toward the first house beyond the small community, and Max parked well down the road. "The owner may not be able to see us clearly from his front window, but that dirt track is filled with potholes and barely passable," he said. "Let's get out of the car here and go up a little closer on foot."

As the propane tank by the side of the house came into clear view, Max stopped. Several sheep and goats were in a log corral behind the house. The front door—there was no porch—was visible from their vantage point. "He'll see us soon. I'm sure he heard us coming up the road. He'd have to—"

Kris suddenly hurled herself at Max, knocking him to the ground. As they hit the dirt, a shot rang out and a bullet struck a fence post near where Max had been standing.

"What the—" he managed, then ducked again as another shot ran out.

"How did you know—" he sputtered, still catching his breath.

"I heard a shell being fed into a rifle chamber," she whispered.

"You come to steal my goats? Not anymore," the man called out. "Get off my land!"

Max focused on the white-haired Navajo man who'd appeared from behind the rear of the house and was standing a few feet from the propane tank. Seeing that Kris had drawn her weapon, he shook his head quickly. "No guns. If we set off that propane, we'll all be blown to hell."

She did as he asked but kept her eyes on the Navajo man holding the lever action rifle.

"*Yáat'ééh*, uncle," Max called out in greeting, keeping his voice steady. "We didn't come to harm you or your animals. We were just hoping you could help us find someone."

"If you're from that uranium company, just get out of here. I'm not letting anyone go looking for that yellow dirt on my land, and you can't scare me by poisoning my livestock. I'm not giving up my land and you can't drive me away. I'll shoot you if you try."

"No, uncle, we're not with the uranium mines. We work for the tribe."

"Then stand up and come over where I can see you. The shadows are getting long, and I want to see who I'm talking to."

"Do you think he's setting us up?" Kris studied the elderly man holding the rifle, then added, "Those trees do put us in the shadow, but even so he nearly scored a hit."

"If what you really mean is that he almost shot off a chunk of my head, you're right," Max muttered.

"Come on over or I'll start shooting again," the man warned.

"Let's take a chance," Kris said, then stood up and started

walking toward the man, her hands out far from her body to show she wasn't armed.

Cursing, Max scrambled to his feet and caught up to her. "Are you crazy? You're a *biagáana!*" he said, hurrying in front of her and shielding her.

"So? He's undoubtedly seen a white person before," she answered with a quick half smile.

A few tense minutes passed as the man looked them over. Then at long last he put down his rifle and invited them inside with a wave of his hand.

Kris and Max entered the small wood-framed home. The living room held a chair and an old sofa. The pillow in the middle replaced a missing cushion. The woodstove in the corner was lit, even though it was probably still sixty-five degrees outside.

Max loosened his jacket and glanced over at Kris, who was doing the same.

"I don't get much company," the man said, then invited them to make themselves comfortable.

They sat on the couch, using the cushions on either side of the pillow.

When their host offered them some herbal tea, Max and Kris accepted. The herbal mixture was pleasant to the taste, and soothing. "This is very good," Kris said, "and sweet."

"I make it with what your people call beard tongue. Here, we call it hummingbird food. It's a drink my grandmother taught me to make many years ago. I still pick the plants the way she taught me, too. When I take what I need, I explain to the plant left behind why I'm picking its neighbor. Then I leave pollen as an offering. That way I can continue to walk in beauty," he added.

As their host sipped his drink, Max allowed the silence to stretch. Interrupting it would have been seen as rude.

Kris, unused to long stretches of silence, shifted uncomfortably but also remained quiet.

At long last Max spoke. "Uncle, we're searching for a man who collects firewood and lives in this area. Recently, he saw something…unpleasant and frightening."

"The Anglo woman," he said with a nod. "My neighbor is putting his money together to have an Enemy Way done. He hasn't been himself since that day." He stared out the window. "But I should warn you. He's not letting anyone come to his home now—especially young Anglo women," he said, looking at Kris, and adding, "And he's a better shot than I am, too."

"Could you let him know that we're coming and ask him not to shoot?" Kris asked, remembering not to make eye contact.

He shook his head. "He has no phone. Neither do I. I'd go with you, but I can't leave my flock. Some of my neighbors have been finding some of their sheep dead each morning. That's why we're keeping them closer, particularly at night. There's talk that maybe someone from the mining company is poisoning them. But sheep die naturally, too, so I don't know if there's any truth to that." He gave them directions where to go find the old man. "He goes by the name K'osnézí."

As they left the home, Kris glanced at Max. "What's that nickname mean?"

"Long neck," Max answered.

As her gaze took in the surrounding area, she sighed. "And here I thought that everything looked so peaceful. That just goes to show that there's always more going on than what the eye can see."

He thought of his gift…maybe he *should* try again. But right now all he wanted to do was take a few minutes to rest and gather his strength again. When he'd hit the dirt, avoiding the old man's bullet, he'd landed on his injured side.

Kris glanced at him. "You're in pain. I can see it on your face. What's wrong?"

He told her in clipped sentences. Then, reading the concern on her face, added, "You probably saved my life back there and risked your own in the process. I owe you."

"Don't feel too indebted. I intend to collect," she said, teasing him gently.

He laughed, winced and threw her the keys. "You take the wheel while I lean back awhile. There's a safe house near here. I'll give you directions."

Chapter Thirteen

They had been on the road only about fifteen minutes when he found himself able to breathe freely again. "Find a place to pull over to the shoulder. I'm feeling better now and I'd like to stretch a bit."

"This looks like a good, safe place to take a short walk. There's plenty of trees and brush to hide in, and some big boulders for cover. Hopefully we won't come across anyone else who shoots first and asks questions later."

"You have to remember that traditionalists, by and large, don't have phones and can't call 911. So they take care of themselves."

She pulled off the highway beside a graveled road with a cattle guard. Moments later, she fell into step beside him as they walked parallel to the highway, then stepped into a narrow arroyo where a culvert ran beneath the highway. There was a small stream running in the middle of the low area, probably fed by a spring in the side of the hill farther up. "Are you sure you're going to be okay?" she asked.

The genuine concern in her voice tugged at him, awakening other needs. "I'm fine."

As they turned a corner in the deepening arroyo, she stopped, leaned against a massive boulder and regarded him thoughtfully.

Max saw the gentleness and concern mirrored in her eyes. The ache it left inside him made him realize how badly he needed both in his life. "When you look at me like you're doing right now, you make me feel all crazy inside," he growled. "I want to…"

"To what?" she managed in a whisper, her heart lodged at her throat.

"I can't keep fighting this. And maybe I shouldn't even try." He narrowed the gap between them, leaned down, and took her mouth. His kiss was gentle at first, then turned ruthless, demanding and giving all at the same time.

She surrendered to him as naturally as the water trickling slowly past them, nourishing the desert. Heat pounded through him as fierce urges raged.

Kris sighed, letting him set the pace, following him down the fiery path he'd blazed open. Wild longings she'd never known before heated her blood until minutes became eternities swathed in pleasure.

He drew back to take a breath, his gaze drinking in her face as he caressed the underside of her breast with his palm. "Your heartbeat is telling me that you need me as much as I need you."

She did want him, but her inner voice screamed at her to stop. Something vital was missing—a piece her soul cried out for, insisting to be heard. She wasn't made for casual sex. Her heart couldn't be given halfway. She couldn't open her body to his until the day came when neither of them would feel hesitant to use that most powerful of all words—*love*.

"We're not ready," she said, her voice trembling. As she moved back, he reached for her hand.

"We are," he murmured, bringing her pulse point to his lips. His tongue slid over it in an endless searing circle. "Listen to your heart. It's whispering to you. My body in yours. Together…we'll complete each other."

Kris couldn't breathe. His eyes smoldered as they held

hers, and his wildness called to her to drop her caution, to take life as it came.

Yet what he was offering her wasn't enough. She needed…more. "I want you, Max, you already know that," she said, moving away with halting steps. "But a fling won't satisfy me, no matter how pleasurable, not in the long run. Sooner or later, there would be regrets that would taint everything we shared. Deep inside, you know that, too."

He caressed her face with the palm of his hand. "You want to see my soul before you'll welcome me inside you. But I can give you pleasures that'll make you forget everything else."

His words made new fires erupt through her. For a moment she couldn't even take a breath. "I can't surrender to a shadow," she managed at last.

He wound his arm around her waist and pulled her closer until she could feel his heat. "You wouldn't feel a shadow when I move inside you. I'm a man…a man who wants you."

Her body felt liquid, and she felt herself drowning in the power of those eyes that were blazing into hers. "No," she whispered in a trembling voice.

This time Max made no move to bridge the gap between them. "One day you'll understand the power of what's ours to share. Our bodies will bind us, making their own rules."

Kris wanted to throw caution to the wind, to forget everything and simply let him take her now. But to have more, she'd have to do with less…for now.

They ended up walking farther up the wash, finding a small, deep pool against the hillside where water emerged between layers of rocks. A cool breeze was blowing across the valley to the west, and they could see the sun slowly sinking in the sky.

Max glanced down at the medicine pouch on his belt. "A medicine man I know made me promise to always keep the *jish* with me, and I have…for all the good it does. If it would do something useful like stop physical pain, or even the one inside me, it wouldn't be so bad."

"Maybe it needs time to work," she said softly. "These days everyone wants instant gratification, but all too often we appreciate the things that require patience much more."

"You're not at all like your sister. She lived in the 'now,' and didn't believe in waiting for what she wanted."

Kris smiled. "She went into her marriages—and out of them—the same way, too." After a long pause, she added, "The thing about her is that she was happiest by herself. I honestly don't think she ever needed anyone else."

"But *you* needed her," he observed.

Kris nodded. "She was my older sister, and my only living relative. I had hoped we could be a real family again," she said. "But, in the long run she probably wouldn't have been comfortable with that. Closeness wasn't her thing. Like you, she liked keeping people at arm's length."

"Our line of work requires that certain doors remain closed to everyone outside of ourselves. But disappointment in the eyes of someone you care about can be hard to take. It's easier not to let anyone get too close in the first place."

She could sense that he was talking about himself, not just Tina. She moved closer to his side, matching his strides, not touching him but letting him get a feel for the partnership that already existed between them. "The very wall you think protects you can also become a prison. Job-related secrets are one thing, whether you're a police officer, a marine or a businessman with proprietary information. But not everything about you fits into that category," Kris said, looking into his eyes. "Let me see who you are, Max. I deserve your trust. Show me that there's room in your heart for more than secrets…that there's room for me."

Stopping, he cupped her face in his hands, and looked into her eyes. "You know I care. But there are things about me that are hard to explain." He exhaled loudly and moved away. "Nothing much scares me, but you know what does? I'm afraid of what I'll see on your face once you know precisely who and what I am."

"I won't judge you, Max. We've been through too much for that. In your heart you already know this."

He chose a big rock near the stream and sat down. Kris joined him, shifting so that they were face-to-face.

Max remained quiet for quite some time and she could sense the struggle going on inside him. Knowing that the next step was up to him, she waited…and hoped.

"This means a lot to you so I'll tell you what you want to know," he said slowly. "But in the end, you may find it even more unsettling." Max took a breath, then began. "Two years ago the son of our tribal president was taken from his parents— kidnapped. Up to then, I'd been a police detective with the Farmington P.D. and very happy at the job. But that one investigation changed everything." He ran a hand through his hair and gazed at some indeterminate point off in the distance.

Seconds felt like lifetimes as Kris waited for him to continue. Then, at long last, he spoke again.

"The search involved several agencies, not just the tribal police and the FBI. One of the suspects was spotted at a gas station in the San Juan Mountains in southern Colorado, so we all concentrated on that area. We threw out our jurisdictional issues, banded together, and soon afterwards we caught the kidnappers, holed up in a mountain cabin." He took a deep breath. "But then we discovered that the boy had gotten away from them the night before. The kidnappers had already been out looking for him when our officers made the arrest."

As he lapsed into another long, tense silence, Kris took his hand and kept it in hers. Her touch reassured him, telling him without words that she wouldn't judge him.

Slowly his gaze shifted back to her, losing its faraway quality as his thoughts returned to the present, and he continued the story. "Navajo trackers were brought in because they're the best, but even they couldn't pick up his trail. The decision was then made to send in teams to work the area along the river, thinking the kid would go downstream, trying to find his way back to a settlement." He paused. "But I'd grown up in the those mountains and knew they were covered with gold and silver mines dating back to the early nineteen hundreds. I was convinced that an eight-year-old boy would hole up at night, worried about falling into one of those mines. Of course he'd also want to stay away from the riverbanks where he could be easily spotted by the kidnappers.

"That's the reason why, instead of working the area right by the river where most of the others were, I elected to search the woods. The kid was smart, I already knew that, so I chose a section beyond the far bank because that would have put a barrier between him and the kidnappers who'd be out looking for him."

"That was good thinking," she agreed. "Trying to get inside his head, that is."

"I thought so, too, but the lack of a trail had the experts convinced that I was searching the wrong place. I kept at it anyway. Eventually, I managed to pick up signs that told me the kid had skillfully been wiping out his own tracks with a leafy branch. I used the radio to call for more teams, but, by then it was getting dark. The search was called off until the next dawn."

She squeezed his hand, signaling for him to continue.

"I was on my way back when I found a mine—the hard way—falling through some hidden boards. I managed to catch myself and break my fall, but I ended up slicing my palm on a rock outcropping with a lot of sharp quartz crystals." A shadow crossed his face as the memories rushed through him. "As I was getting my hand loose, I dislodged a crystal, which remained stuck in my hand. By then, my hand and the crystal were soaked in blood. I was sitting there, back on solid ground and catching my breath, when I noticed how the starlight was playing on the crystal, making it glow."

He took a deep, unsteady breath, his expression showing the toll taken by the excruciating images flashing through his mind's eye. When he looked at her again, his gaze was intensely personal and filled with a vulnerability she hadn't known he possessed. "I can't explain how it happened, but suddenly my spirit traveled up the mountain. I saw the old wooden buildings and the area of waste rock where mining operations had left a gash in the mountainside. There were boards up there, too, with a gap revealing a vertical shaft and a broken ladder inside."

He swallowed, pulled his hand away from hers and balled it into a fist. He then continued in a deliberately even tone she knew was meant to conceal his emotions. "The vision ended then, but I was sure I knew where the boy was. I told no one—I was afraid that I'd gone crazy—but I went up there that night anyway. I pulled away the boards, found the kid, and got him out of that mine."

"He was okay?"

Max nodded. "It turned out that he'd hidden in a mine, made his way almost to the top of a vertical shaft, then discovered the ladder was too short to climb out. He couldn't go back down because he'd broken some of the rungs climbing up. He was trapped where he was. I had to pull him out."

"That kid must have been so happy to see you!" she said with deep conviction.

"He was, and so were the others when I brought him back. But in the next few days everything changed," he said, his voice cold and detached as if he'd distanced himself from the account. "The boy told the others that he'd been too afraid to yell, so people began to question how I'd figured out his location. I decided to tell the truth."

"But people didn't believe you," she said, feeling his frustration.

He shrugged, weariness mirrored on his face. "The tribal president and his family were so grateful they stood behind me without question, but it wasn't long before I knew I had to leave the force. Half of the officers suspected I'd been involved with the kidnappers somehow, the others thought I was nuts, or on peyote. Either way I was screwed because no one wanted to work with me."

"But my sister did," she added quietly.

"She stood by me," he confirmed. "After I quit, I fell apart for a while. Mentally, I was in a very dark place. It was your sister who helped me climb back out of that pit. She insisted that I go find a medicine man who knew about things like that. In fact, she ended up driving me there."

"Was that the same medicine man who advised you to carry the medicine pouch?" she asked, pointing.

"Yes. The crystal that pierced my hand that day is inside it, along with pollen and other collected substances. But the thing is, I've never had another vision, not since that day. And I've tried hard to make it happen. I've been hoping to find out where your sister hid that platinum. But I just can't make it work."

"You're not comfortable with it. Maybe that's part of the problem. If you're ever really pressed to use your gift, I bet you'd find a way."

He gave her a surprised look. "Your sister said much the same thing to me. But I still think it was the kind of thing that happens once in a lifetime."

"And you're relieved," she commented gently. "I can hear it in your voice."

"Yeah, maybe I am," he admitted. "So now you know about me. The question is, do you still trust me, or do you think I'm a total wacko?" His gaze stayed on her, probing.

"You are who you are—a friend and my partner. Those are the only labels I'm interested in." She sat back and regarded him thoughtfully. "And now that you're no longer with the police department, you've got a different kind of investigative job. How did you end up with the job you've got now?"

"Some secrets aren't mine to share, but I will tell you that my work for the tribe suits me. It's the kind of job I was born to do."

"You love it as much as I do my plants," she observed quietly.

He nodded. "I help restore the balance."

"I'm a strong believer in fate," she said, "and I'm beginning to think the reason I came into your life is because you needed someone who could help you accept what's inside you. Some of the best things life has to offer go beyond what the eye can see."

"Or maybe I'm meant to teach you to focus on reality," he answered with a teasing grin. "There's something to be said for that, too." He turned to look up at the trees, extending his arms to the sky and stretching his muscles.

"How are you feeling now?" she asked.

"Ready to get back to work. Let's try to find the old man again. Are you up for it?"

"That depends. Do you think we'll get shot at again?" she asked wryly.

"Navajos take the possibility of someone hurting their sheep very, very seriously, so we might just hear a bullet or two flying overhead again." He started back to the SUV. "But this time we'll be watching."

Chapter Fourteen

A half hour later, as they neared a solitary hogan in the canyon ahead, Max's senses were on full alert. He wouldn't get caught unawares again.

"That hogan looks smaller than the others we've seen," she commented.

"It's the kind that's used just for ceremonies. There's a residence farther ahead between those pines," he said, pointing it out. "But a lot of our people still live in hogans that are like that, only a bit larger."

"I've seen them from the outside only—the log sides, the smoke holes and the blankets over the entrances. But what are they like on the inside?" she asked.

"Sparse—a few sheepskins on the ground and a wood-stove for cooking and heat. Maybe shelves for food and cooking utensils, and a cooler or two for keeping ice for milk and eggs. Light often comes from oil or kerosene lamps and lanterns." He sighed. "Poverty is a way of life on the Rez. Sheep and goats provide wool and meat. There's nothing like freshly made mutton stew and a soft rug to sit on. There's a lot to be said for a traditionalist's way of life."

As they approached to within a hundred yards, Max slowed down to a crawl, inching forward in the SUV. "We need to let him know we're friends, even from a distance," he said. "I've got an idea. When we get out of the vehicle, I'm going to start singing a *Hozonji*."

"What's that?" she asked.

"It's what my people call a Song of Blessing. There are many kinds of *Hozonjis*. Usually, they're passed down through families from one generation to the next. The song, depending on its nature, can be used for a variety of things. Of course if they're used too often, their power is lost."

"The power of the spoken word—or a name."

"Exactly."

Max parked about twenty yards from the hogan, facing the door. Although he'd parked in the open, cover was right behind them and to either side.

Kris was in no hurry to leave the concealment of the SUV, but following Max's lead, stepped out, allowing herself to be seen yet staying behind her open door.

Before she could speak, Max's voice rose in the air, breaking the stillness around them. She didn't understand the words, but the song reverberated with the power of the desert and the strength of a tribe that had surmounted countless obstacles.

Max's voice was clear and strong, and its masculine timber sent its vibrations through her, touching her heart in ways she'd never imagined possible.

It was then that she suddenly understood what was happening between them. Despite all the reasons not to, she was falling in love with Max Natoni.

As the last note of Max's song echoed in the quiet that followed, she waited, scarcely breathing. All her senses were alive, drinking in the peace that remained in the wake of his song.

"What's the song about?" she asked, her voice whisper-soft.

He came over and stood beside her. "It's a prayer to the Holy Mountains, the guardians of the Navajo People. It invokes their protection."

"Even the insects were quiet when you sang it. It resonated with…power."

Max looked at her, his eyes vibrant and burning with an inner fire that almost took her breath away. "The song was a gift from my father to me. It was a part of him and now it's a part of me."

Sensations she couldn't even describe laced around her. Though danger surrounded them, the power of his song lingered in the air. It spoke to her, reassuring her and asking her to trust in a way of life that called to her, although she didn't understand it.

Her gaze on him, she began to understand other things, too. Max needed her—and she needed him. Together they *were* stronger. Instinct rooted in woman's intuition told her that Max would surrender to that truth someday, too. Although the road ahead would be filled with pitfalls and danger, together they were more than a match for whatever came their way.

"What's going through your mind, pretty lady?" he whispered, turning toward her.

Spellbound, she felt herself drowning in the power of the feelings he'd awakened in her, but suddenly a voice called out and Max looked away. The magic of the moment broken, she brushed aside the sense of loss that enveloped her and focused on the job at hand.

"*Yáat'ééh,* uncle," Max answered.

A minute later, they were invited to approach. They came within twenty feet when the man suddenly backed up a step. He howled one word in terror, then raced over to his truck, an older model green pickup with high wooden sides around the bed.

"No, no, it's okay," Max shouted. But nothing could stop the man now.

He started the engine, clashed though the gears in panic, then sped away down the road, leaving a heavy trail of dust like a giant tail.

They ran back to the SUV, but, after a few miles, it was clear they'd lost track of him.

"He knows this area like the back of his hand," Max said, slowing to a normal speed. "He wanted to get away from us, and he did."

"What the heck happened?" she asked, "Everything was going so well! We waited until he waved us in, then, in the blink of an eye he suddenly freaked out. What was that he yelled?"

"*Chindi,*" he said quietly.

"I don't understand. Didn't you tell me that was the word for spirit, the evil kind?"

Max nodded. "I think what got to him was the physical resemblance between you and your sister. At a distance you two *do* look a lot alike. My guess is that his vision isn't very sharp in subdued light and he thought the *chindi* had found him."

"What do we do now?" she asked, suddenly very tired.

"We'll try again in a day or so, but next time you stay in the car. Right now I'm going to make a call and see if I can get hold of a computer. I have an idea I'm working on, and I need access to certain things." Without elaborating, he took out his cell phone but found he couldn't get a signal. Stepping out of the car, he walked uphill a few yards, then gave her a thumb's-up.

He returned minutes later. "We're going to a Chapter House over in Wheatfields."

"What kind of house?"

"Chapter Houses are the heart of local government here on the Rez. Since there are no meetings scheduled today it'll be locked up, but someone I know will meet us there and let us in."

"All right," she said.

As Max drove down the graveled road she said nothing. Frustration was tearing at her, undermining her confidence and making her doubt their strategy.

"We've been nearly kidnapped, chased, run from and shot at, but we're still no closer to finding my sister's killer," she said after several moments. "Do you realize that? Harris and Talbot continue to elude us, and the platinum that she died protecting is still out there somewhere."

"You're tired—with reason. It's been a long day, longer even than yesterday, and it'll be a while before we get any real downtime. But don't let fatigue get to you. That never leads to anything good."

She didn't answer. He was right and she knew it. She'd worked for twenty-four-hour stretches several times overseas. In the Corps, they'd called what she was experiencing now combat stress reaction. When human beings didn't get enough sleep, and were constantly on edge, they started to unravel. That usually led to stupid mistakes that got them killed.

"When we first started I was so sure I could find answers, but so far…" She hadn't meant to speak the words out loud, but now it was too late to take them back. "The thing is, I can't remember anything about this part of the reservation that would have made it particularly significant to my sister or me. Yet there's that one-word message—'remember.' I've done nothing but think about that, but for the life of me, I still can't figure out what she meant by it."

"I don't have the answer to that, either, but I know your sister had something specific in mind."

As they headed west toward the Chapter House, weaving their way along the dirt roads in the foothills, Max glanced over at her. "You now know a great deal about me. So, for the sake of balance, how about telling me something about yourself that most people don't know?"

Kris made a show of looking around. "Are we there yet?" she asked.

He burst out laughing. "So, you have your own secrets, too."

"Anyone who serves in a war zone returns with a few secrets—and nightmares," she said somberly. "But that's all in my past. I prefer to dwell in the present."

"Despite the bullets flying around?"

"It's not the bullets that frighten me most. It's what'll happen if we don't find answers."

"The platinum is important to the tribe, but if we don't

find it, we'll move on. What about you? Do you think you can do the same?"

"No. Giving up isn't an option," she said. "I have to see this through for Tina's sake and mine. She and I both lived by a code of honor. It's an outdated concept, I know, but sometimes honor and loyalty are all we have left at the end of the day. If I turn my back on her memory now, I'll forfeit a piece of myself—the center that defines who I am."

He nodded, understanding.

"By going after my sister, they made one very bad enemy—me."

"Two," Max said, correcting her.

She nodded. "Yes, two enemies who'll work together to become their worst nightmare."

THEY ARRIVED AT A MODERN stucco building perched against a hillside southwest of Shiprock a short time later. The grounds were well maintained, and a new model pickup was parked in front of a log barrier on the left side of the parking lot.

"Our contact should be around here somewhere," he said.

"Is that him?" she asked, pointing ahead. A tall Navajo man in his late thirties with wide shoulders and a lean build was walking up concrete steps leading to a side door, duffel bag in hand.

"That's him," he said, recognizing Smoke as he got out of the SUV.

"Who is he?" she asked, following his lead.

"I don't know his real name. But that's not unusual here on the Rez where nicknames are far more common."

"Yet you still trust him?" she asked.

"With my life—like you would with another marine."

His answer told her far more than his words had. This was undoubtedly another member of the group he belonged to. "So what will you be doing in there, exactly?" she asked.

"I want to do a comprehensive background check on Talbot.

From the beginning, Harris covered his tracks, knowing exactly what he was doing and how to do it. So the key is Talbot, who wanted to work both sides of the theft. If I dig deep enough, I may get a lead that'll tell us where to find him."

"That's a good idea, but the kind of Internet digging you're talking about requires access to special databases."

"I'll have what I need," he said flatly. "I also plan to get help tracking down the old man. We need people working the area, checking houses and along the roads. I'm going to have some friends of mine start asking around for him. Navajos usually like talking to other Navajos, so a low-key approach will help us."

The door to the Chapter House had been left unlocked. Max went in first and headed to a small meeting room off to the left where a desktop computer had been set up. Before she could follow him in, the Navajo man she'd seen before came out of another room across the hall and blocked her way.

His face was stony, and he pointed with his lips to the bag he'd carried. "It doesn't weigh much. Will you take it to the woman up the way? She's sitting outside her house, weaving."

She tried to step around him to go talk to Max, who was already at the computer, but the man blocked her again.

"She's elderly and the sheepskins inside the bag will ease the pain in her joints," he added.

"Max?" she called out.

"This'll take me awhile. If you want to go for a walk, it's fine. You'll be safe around here."

She took a deep breath, trying to curb her temper as the Navajo man gestured to the bag again. Although tempted to throw it at him, she picked it up and walked outside. Max had told her that Navajos loved to talk. Maybe woman-to-woman she'd be able to learn something useful.

Once outside Kris glanced around. The house in the direction the man had nodded was the next building up the road, just a hundred yards away.

As Kris approached the elderly woman, who was seated before her vertical loom at the rear of the house, she could hear her singing softly. Her lined face looked completely at peace as her strong hands spun magic. Kris didn't interrupt, but sat on the ground, within the woman's peripheral vision and listened, waiting to be invited to approach. The light was fading now and the woman would soon have to stop for the day.

When the woman finished, she looked over and waved at Kris, welcoming her to come up. Kris brought the bag closer and placed it by her. "I was asked by a man at the Chapter House to bring these sheepskins to you," she said, then helped the woman pull them carefully out of the bag.

The weaver laid them out, picked the one that looked thickest, then set it in front of the loom. Spreading her long skirt around herself, she sat down again and made herself comfortable with a contented sigh. "My legs get very stiff these days, but the sheepskins help."

"The song you were singing was beautiful," Kris said.

"It's a weaving song. When we weave, we're taught to keep our thoughts happy and peaceful. Then our work unfolds in the right way and becomes part of the weaver's heart and mind."

Kris came closer to take a better look. "It's such a gorgeous design!" she said in awe.

"This is what we call a Storm Rug. In the middle, here," she said, pointing with her lips, "is my home. The four rectangles in the corners represent the four sacred mountains that guard the *Diné Bekayah*, the Navajo homeland. The zigzag lines represent lightning and connect all the elements to the center of the rug."

The colors and design gave the rug an energy all its own. The bright red color was reminiscent of a desert sunrise. She thought of Max's code name, Thunder. The vibrancy of the rug reminded her of him—lines that flowed and merged with the passion of lightning. The weaver had created a design that portrayed all the freedom of nature and yet held the symmetry of Navajo life.

"Thank you for explaining the design to me. Knowing makes the rug even more beautiful to me. It's…just perfect," she said at last.

The weaver shook her head. "No, not perfect. Every rug must have a break in the pattern. It frees the weaver's mind. Otherwise her thoughts become trapped in the blanket. Spider Woman taught Changing Woman the way to weave and she, in turn, taught others. The skill came from them and has been handed down through the generations."

The weaver obviously had a deep knowledge of symbols. Remembering the one carved into the doorway of the house they'd stayed at, she crouched on the sand and traced it on the ground.

"Have you ever seen this symbol? I think it's of Navajo origin."

The weaver studied the design Kris had drawn. "That's part of a story my mother told me once a long, long time ago," she said softly. "We hold our stories dear. They're part of us, you see," she added, "but I'll share this one with you."

With a faraway look in her eyes, the weaver gazed at the sacred mountains, now covered in the brilliant orange and red hues of sunset. "It took about three years after the Long Walk before we were finally allowed to return to our land. By then, years of near starvation had worn down our people. When we came home to our land between the sacred mountains, our enemies were everywhere. Desperation defeated the spirit of many. It was then that a secret band of our strongest men joined together to protect the ones who couldn't fight for themselves. They were known as the Brotherhood of Warriors. They remained in the shadows, bound by honor, protecting the tribe. No one knew who they were, but all felt the results of their work.

"Slowly the tribe gained strength, and hope, and thrived once again. What you have drawn there," she said glancing down, "was their symbol—the sign of the Brotherhood. It was said that to become one of the circle, a man would have to undergo a trial by fire that would test his spirit. Fire purifies and cleanses. Only the best were equal to the challenge."

"Brotherhood of Warriors...."

"Of course a legend like that can grow out of hope alone," the weaver said with an easy smile. "No one really knows if the Brotherhood ever existed, and these days it's just one of many stories our people tell our young to inspire them. Life can be very hard here on the *Dinétah*."

Kris knew she'd found her answer. The Brotherhood wasn't mythical. She knew one of its members—maybe even two. Now, at long last, she understood Max and why he was keeping secrets from her. He loved this land where hardship and magic went hand-in-hand. It was here on this Rez, where tears had given way to new strength, that Max truly belonged.

Kris pulled one of her new business cards from her wallet. "When you're finished with this rug, if it's ever for sale, call me. I'd like to buy it."

"Thank you. I make my living selling my rugs, so I'd be happy to contact you," she answered, taking Kris's card. "Walk in beauty."

"Walk in beauty," Kris responded, getting to her feet. The heartbeat of the Navajo Nation was in the power those words held.

Chapter Fifteen

By the time she returned to the Chapter House, the sun had set and Max and his Navajo companion were outside on the steps.

After some hurried words in Navajo, Max motioned her toward the SUV. "Ready to go?"

"Where to?"

"I now have a lead to Talbot," he said. "It turns out that he owns an investment company. I checked for properties under that firm's name and found one about an hour and a half from here." He unlocked the SUV and they climbed inside. "It's a farmhouse east of Bloomfield along the river valley. The location's perfect since Harris and Talbot are undoubtedly looking for a place to crash and regroup where nobody's likely to notice them. We can get there by six-thirty, depending on traffic."

IT WAS DARK WHEN THEY passed by the house, which was located about a quarter mile north of the highway behind an apple orchard. There weren't any visible lights on, and if there was a vehicle parked by the house, they couldn't see from the distance.

Once they'd passed the long driveway leading to the building, Max pulled off beside the highway. "Let's go up for a closer look. This time I want you to drive. If we need to take action in a hurry, I'll be armed and ready. Just make sure that you put the engine compartment between you and the perps if we have to make a quick stop."

"But that'll put *you* on their side," she said.

"Yeah, but if I have to jump out, I'll be able to return fire immediately and not have to worry about watching where I'm going—like into that irrigation ditch on the driver's side. Meanwhile, you'll still have some protection."

A few minutes later, Kris was at the wheel, driving slowly up the graveled lane. The rural setting accentuated the darkness, and the orchard on her right only served to conceal what lay ahead. For a moment she found herself looking along the shoulder for signs of disturbed ground—and IEDs.

They had their windows down, listening for any sign of human activity, but all they could hear were crickets beside the road and the crunch of the tires on gravel. "Just another hundred yards, and we'll be there. Cut the lights completely now," Max said.

Kris reached over for the knob and turned off their parking lights, slowing down a little more. "Overseas, I rode down roads like these wondering if I'd ever make it home with my own legs and arms still intact. I never figured I'd come home to the same thing."

Suddenly a powerful engine roared to life from somewhere up ahead, and they were blinded by headlights coming directly at them. There was a loud pop and a simultaneous blast of gunfire as bullets struck the windshield.

"Get off the road!" Max yelled, crouching low to the side.

"No fooling!" she answered as more glass shattered, spraying them with jagged cubes.

Kris instinctively threw up her free arm to protect her face, swung the wheel to the right, brushed a tree, then bounced back to the left.

"Hang on," she shouted, realizing the ditch was their only escape. Fighting the wheel to keep them upright, she hit the brakes and eased over the edge.

They dropped off quickly, tipping hard just as the onrushing truck struck them a glancing blow.

Feeling the front end dropping away, she desperately swung the wheel back to the right, grabbing for road. It was like trying to hang onto air. They rolled over onto the driver's side, screeching and sliding for several feet, then came to a hard stop.

Kris smashed her head against something, nearly blacking out from the pain. When her thoughts cleared, she could hear Max yelling at her.

"They're coming back. Can you get out?"

Her left arm was numb, and she was having a hard time feeling her hand. Something warm, probably blood, was flowing down her left temple. "Can't reach my seat-belt release. It's the steering wheel…it's pushing me into the backrest."

There was a metallic thump, and a gunshot. "They're trying to pin us down," he said. "Stay still. I'll get you out."

Kris smelled the acrid scent of gasoline mingling with hot motor oil. Suddenly she flashed back to a narrow dirt track continents away. Their vehicle had been hit by an RPG just in front of the driver's feet, and she could hear his screams as the fuel started to burn. His pleas as he'd begged her to get him out were indelibly etched in her mind.

She'd been seated in the back, and had been able to push her door open. She'd scrambled out and managed to get a fire extinguisher off the rack, but it had been like spitting on a volcano. The subsequent blast had knocked her halfway across the road.

He'd cried out one more time—an inhuman scream that still rang in her nightmares.

"I can't, I can't get any closer!" Kris called out to him, suddenly back there again.

"What? Kris, keep trying. I'll keep them back!" Max called to her.

Max, his seat belt undone, reached up to the handle, pushing the door up and away with a mighty heave. Using the center console as a footrest, he lifted himself out of the SUV and swung around onto the road.

Looking back toward the highway, he saw the big truck turning around. The headlights were suddenly aimed right at them, but the vehicle wasn't moving. Somebody in the passenger's side fired two more shots, the bullets whining overhead.

"Down on the ground, Natoni," Harris ordered.

Max ran around to the front of the SUV, his pistol out as more bullets ricocheted off the road where he'd been a few seconds ago. He looked at the shattered windshield, and Kris who was lying there behind it, her seat belt still in place.

"Run. If this catches fire, it'll take us both out," Kris said, her thoughts clearing. It wasn't back then, it was *now,* and she wouldn't allow Max to die along with her. "Lead them away. Hide in the orchard," she said. "It's your only chance."

"Can you move at all?" he asked, bending low and tilting his head so he could see her expression.

"I can—" she said, but before she could finish, Harris started shooting again. "Go!" she yelled to him. "If the engine catches fire…."

"Hang on," he said, then, taking careful aim around the side of the SUV, he shot out one of Harris's headlights. Suddenly the area was considerably dimmer.

Staying on the ground, Max fired two more rounds, but he missed the remaining headlight. It was enough, though. Whoever was behind the wheel threw the truck into Reverse and started backing up. Reaching the highway, the truck whipped around and drove off with screeching tires.

They were plunged into a yawning darkness. "Kris, don't give up," Max called out to her. "Can you close your eyes and protect your face with your arm? I'm going to break out the windshield and reach in for you."

"Okay, go ahead."

Max took off his jacket and, using it to protect his hands, pulled out the glass in chunks, creating a hole as it crumbled away. Soon he'd created a big opening on the driver's side. After breaking away some of the jagged edges with the butt of his pistol, he reached in.

Kris was lying on her side, half-turned toward the passenger door, staring across at him. Her face was bloodied and he could see the fear and pain in her eyes. "I'm getting you out of there." Shaken, he pushed at the release button of her seat belt with renewed determination.

The mechanism refused to yield. Max took out his lockback pocket knife and cut the seat-belt strap in half. After that, it took some maneuvering, but he finally managed to pull her out.

As he hauled Kris to her feet, they heard a hissing sound. "Time's up," she said in a faraway voice.

In one fluid motion, he lifted her into his arms and ran headlong down the road into the darkness. About thirty yards from the car something like an iron fist stopped him in his tracks. There was a brilliant flash of light and heat and, in an instant, they were knocked onto their backs.

"What the…" Max rolled away from Kris and looked back at the wrecked car. It was illuminated, but not from its own explosion or fire. The flames, smoke and rubble clouding the air were all coming from Talbot's house or, more properly, from where it had once been.

He looked down at her arm. A quick inspection revealed no obvious breaks, just a bad bruise and a few scrapes. "Your arm's not broken, but you may have internal injuries."

"No, I'm okay. I slammed my head, and that had me going for a while, but I'm all right," she said. "Right now I just want to get away from here."

He helped her stand up, his gaze returning to Talbot's house. "If there was any evidence inside, it's toast now." He focused back on her. "Cops are going to start arriving in just a few more minutes. We need to leave the area. Can you walk?"

She took a few shaky steps. "Yes, but I can't exactly race

you to the highway," she said. Her legs were bruised and she was still feeling wobbly.

"You won't have to." He saw a white SUV turn up the road, stop, then blink the headlights twice.

He put his gun away, then stepped into view. "Hang back while I check things out, but I believe help has arrived."

"What if it's Harris and Talbot in another vehicle?"

"They won't be coming back, not with the house going up like a torch. This place will be getting a lot of attention before long." He jogged toward the SUV.

A minute later the SUV pulled up behind their wrecked vehicle and Max jumped out of the passenger side. Before she could utter a word of protest, he scooped her into his arms and carried her over to the back seat of the vehicle, setting her gently inside. "Okay, let's roll," he told the driver.

Kris looked back at their vehicle and saw flames licking up around the engine compartment. Black smoke was starting to billow up, and the sight made her turn away. "It's going to blow!" she said. "Hurry!"

The SUV rocketed back down the driveway in Reverse, then whipped around, and within fifteen seconds they were accelerating down the highway.

"Hospital?" the driver asked without turning around.

"Yeah," Max answered. "And anonymity."

Kris knew beyond a shadow of a doubt then that the driver was also one of the Brotherhood. Secure in the knowledge that they were safe, she gave in to the pain thrumming through her body and allowed herself to slip into the welcoming void.

LATER, AFTER SEVERAL groggy minutes at the hospital, where she was subjected to some probing, poking and questions like "what day is this?" Kris was able to drift off into a deep, comforting sleep. By the time she woke again, she was lying in a very comfortable bed in somebody's bedroom. She glanced down at her arm and noticed antiseptic in some shallow cuts and scrapes, and two small bandages on deeper wounds. At least there hadn't been a need for stitches.

Max was standing at the foot of the bed, and he smiled when she looked up at him. "Hey, sunshine. About time you woke up."

"Where are we? Last I remember we were at the hospital."

"You got the once-over, and the doctor pronounced you in good shape, not counting the bruises, cuts and scrapes. He said you'd be sore for a few days, though. Since we couldn't protect you at the hospital and there was no reason for you to stay, you were given a sedative to help you sleep. Then we transported you to this safe house."

As she glanced down at herself she realized that she'd kicked off the sheet, and was wearing only her bra and panties. "Who undressed me?" she asked quickly, pulling up the sheet until it covered her bra.

"I'm going to have to take credit for that burden." He sat beside her on the bed and held her gaze. "You know, I've never seen a bra that pink in all my life."

She glared at him. "Just how many bras have you seen?"

He laughed. "A gentleman never tells."

She reached down to adjust the sheet, but as she moved, the bandage on her arm tugged at her skin. "Ow."

"Are you okay?" he asked, taking her hand gently in both of his.

"I'm just sore," she managed. "Back there…trapped in the car…I held you up and I'm sorry about that. I had a bit of a flashback."

"Don't apologize. But I'm curious. You mentioned not being able to get any closer. What's the story behind that?" he asked.

"My driver," she said quietly. "We were outside the Green Zone in a small convoy, relocating to a new base. An RPG hit our vehicle and the driver was trapped inside, his legs smashed up. I got out, then tried to put out the fire and get him out, but the heat drove me back. I can still hear his screams…." She shuddered, tears running down her face.

Max gazed at her. Though strong as steel, Kris wasn't afraid of her softer, more vulnerable side. She accepted both and ran from neither. That kind of courage was rare and confirmed what he'd known in his heart. Kris was special in every way that mattered to him. That's why he was falling in love with her.

Stunned by the realization, Max gazed at Kris. He couldn't think of anything to do or say, so he just continued to clasp her hand.

"You were under fire, yet you stayed with me. You saved my life," she said softly.

"You gave me quite a scare, Kris. Don't ever do that again," he said in a husky voice.

Hearing a loud crack of thunder outside, she cringed.

"Are you sure you're okay?" he asked quickly.

She nodded. "I'm fine. I just *hate* loud noises. They remind me of things I'd rather forget." She glanced down at herself, searching for a distraction. "Is there someplace I can go wash up?"

"The bathroom is right through that door and there're clothes that may fit you in the closet. Feel free to take whatever you want."

Kris sat up, and he moved toward her. "Let me help."

"No, please don't. If you make it too easy, I'll stop trying. Once I do that, I won't like myself at all," she answered with a smile.

He chuckled softly. It took a person like him who prided his independence to understand someone like her. With effort, he brushed aside the temptation to coddle her.

As she tossed the covers aside, Max held his breath. She was perfectly proportioned, with soft curves that called to a man and skin as smooth as silk. His body tightened. She was courage and vulnerability, softness and toughness, all in one incredible package. He would have given everything to undress her and kiss her senseless right now.

"I need some privacy," Kris said, standing up.

"I'll be in the next room," he said, then memorizing everything about her, walked out.

KRIS WATCHED MAX GO. She'd fantasized about being alone with him in a bedroom, miles away from everything. Of course now that she was, she had black and blue marks everywhere and the scent of gasoline clung to her like glue. She wasn't exactly the stuff of dreams. Max would have had to have been blind with no sense of smell to want her now.

As she remembered the way he'd held her tightly in his arms as he'd carried her to safety, she sighed. Maybe someday...

Kris walked slowly to the closet, opened the door and found a pair of jeans and a shirt she knew would fit her. Laying them across the bed, she went to the bathroom to clean up. The small window there was framed by thin curtains, and the glass was clear, not frosted. She suspected, from the lack of traffic sounds, that this house was in the country, so there was no reason to worry about anyone peering in. It was dark outside, too, so she left the curtains open and didn't give them another thought.

The free-standing tub with its soft blue privacy curtain looked incredibly inviting, and the idea of soaking in hot water became too tempting to resist. Kris washed out her undergarments and hung them up to dry as the tub filled up. She just knew she'd feel much better after a long soak.

She'd placed one leg into the warm water when she heard a scratching sound. As she looked up at the window, a pair of huge yellow eyes peered back at her.

She stepped back quickly, reaching for the shower curtain to cover herself, but the floor was slippery. Desperately trying to break her fall, she grabbed the curtain, hanging on, but the pole came loose from the wall and she fell hard to the floor.

A heartbeat later, Max came crashing into the bathroom. He looked magnificent, wearing nothing but a pair of dark colored briefs. She sucked in her breath and tried to find her voice. "Someone's outside," she managed, pointing.

Without hesitation he ran back out.

Hearing a door being thrown open, she grabbed a terry-cloth robe that was hanging on a hook, wrapped it around herself, then ran into the bedroom. Her pistol was on the nightstand.

Scooping it up, she thumbed off the safety and ran outside the small cabin.

When she reached the corner she found Max standing below a pine, holding a deadly looking ax in his hand. As she walked over, he propped the ax against the outside wall, then pointed up to a branch. "The perp changed locations when he saw me coming."

"Oh, geez!" Staring down at her was a small grey and white owl with enormous yellow eyes. She put her pistol in the pocket of her robe.

Kris looked back at Max, intending to apologize, but as her gaze drifted over his nearly naked body, longing and suppressed needs came crashing to the surface. A shiver coursed up her spine as she saw his body tensing up.

"Don't look at me like that, woman," he growled.

"Moonlight…it does something for you," she whispered.

Max knew he shouldn't touch her. If he did, he'd be lost. Yet destiny called to him, and he knew he had to honor his heart. Seeing Kris tremble as he drew closer was his undoing. There were some things a man was not meant to resist.

Winding his hand around her hair, he lowered his mouth to hers. His kiss was soft at first, but passion heated his blood, compelling him to demand more.

"No one will ever want you more than I do. Feel me. This was meant to be—we were meant to be each other's," he whispered.

The power of his kisses left her senses reeling. She knew that she should pull away but desire held her prisoner in his arms.

Max pulled back her robe, exposing her to his gaze. Using his tongue, he soothed every red and bruised spot covering her body, then slowly traced a trail of fire down her center.

As he lowered himself to his knees and began to give her pleasure, the skies above her rocked with thunder and lightning. Dark delights shattered her. She demanded nothing and welcomed everything.

As her knees weakened, he wrapped his arms around her and lowered her to the ground. She gave herself to him completely, holding nothing back. Her heart had been his and now her body followed.

"We are a part of each other forever now," he murmured as he filled her.

Feelings she had kept locked away in her heart burst to the surface as she felt him deep inside her. The intensity grew with each passing minute as their bodies rocked against each other's, lost in pleasure. Then joining in one glorious moment of release, they drifted over the edge.

Eternities passed before he rolled onto his back, taking her with him. "From now on when you hear thunder, remember this night of love," he whispered in her ear, holding her against him.

His words, so filled with gentleness and caring, comforted her woman's heart.

"To think that I came out ready to shoot those beautiful eyes," she said, looking at the owl, who still hadn't moved.

"Our people say that Owl is a helper to man." He gave her a slow, tender smile. "In this case, I've got to say I agree wholeheartedly."

She sat up slowly, reaching for her robe as a cold breeze blew past them. "The stories…they tie all things Navajo together, don't they?"

"Yes. Stories explain who we are by telling us who we were. We remain strong as a tribe because we honor our past," he said, rising just as a cold sprinkling of rain came down on them.

Inside moments later, Max built a fire. With a warm robe

wrapped comfortably around her, she watched the fireplace, lost in thought. "As a Navajo, you've got a place here on the reservation where you'll always belong. I came back hoping to find the same thing for myself, but I'm not sure that's possible anymore."

"You'll find a way to make it happen once this is over and you go back to your world."

As she heard his words she suddenly wondered if that's how she saw what had happened between them—a temporary surrender to the forces that had brought them together but nothing that would last past tonight.

The possibility saddened her. Yet it wasn't something she was ready to talk to him about. She'd followed her heart. What else was there? The future would unfold at its own pace. She wouldn't worry about it now.

"What's bothering you?" he asked as he helped her to her feet. "I can see in your eyes that something is."

She thought of fairy tale endings and how badly she'd wanted one for herself. "It's nothing," she answered, feeling the weight of the pistol she still carried in her pocket. "I was just thinking of what lies ahead," she added, knowing the case was paramount in his mind and he'd refocus quickly. "You can bet Harris and Talbot have a plan. But I have no idea what to do next. What about you?"

"I'll be working on that late into the night. By morning, I'm hoping our people will come up with a lead that'll take us to where the old man is. Then we'll try to approach him again. But, this time, I want you to leave your hair loose. Since your sister always wore hers in a ponytail, that should help," he said. "But that's the extent of my plans. Experience has taught me that plans lock you in and that can get you killed."

"Not all plans are bad," she answered.

"The only thing elaborate plans get you is a truckload of disappointment."

"Not always. What about all the happily-ever-afters?" she asked, only half jokingly.

"I'm not sure it's in me to believe in those. Life doesn't come with guarantees," he said somberly. "All you can do is live in the moment and do the best you can." Max rubbed his knuckles on her cheek in a light caress, then leaned over for a quick kiss. "Now get some rest. I'll join you soon. But first I need to take care of tribal business."

Chapter Sixteen

Max knew he'd messed up. Although his feelings for Kris were real, he'd had no business making love to her. He had nothing to offer her except uncertainty and a life of secrets she'd never be part of—the very thing she loathed.

He tried to focus on the latest report coming in from the Brotherhood. A quick scan revealed they'd found a lead that would hopefully take him to the old man. After signing off, he glanced at his watch. He'd spent more time in the communications room than he'd realized but, if he was lucky, he might still be able to get some shut-eye before dawn.

Leaving the comm room, he walked down the hall and saw she'd left her door open for him. Max went in silently and gazed down at her. She was sleeping peacefully. Brushing a gentle kiss on her forehead, he forced himself to step back. He didn't trust himself anymore.

Taking a sleeping bag from the closet, he spread it on the floor next to the bed. He needed to be close to her, but this would be enough. As he lay down, he heard the even sounds of her breathing and, at peace for now, drifted off to sleep.

Max awakened shortly after sunrise. To his surprise, she was already up and moving about in the kitchen. The scent of freshly brewed coffee was inviting. He put away his sleeping bag and soon joined her.

Kris glanced at him as he entered the room. "Good morning," she said. "I hope I didn't wake you, but I got hungry."

He saw a plate with big pieces of fry bread, flanked by butter and a jar of honey. There was apple juice on the table, too, and she was busy scrambling eggs.

"The fry bread was in the refrigerator, so I just reheated it in the oven for a few minutes. But I couldn't find any milk, so you'll have to take your coffee black."

"Many Navajos aren't that big on milk. The theory is that cow's milk is for calves."

"That's one argument." She divided the scrambled eggs into two plates, and placed one in front of him. "So what's on the agenda this morning?" she asked in a businesslike tone.

"I have some information we can use to track down the old man. His legal name is Charlie Nez and he'll be delivering a load of firewood this morning. I have the location, but we need to get going soon," he said. "And thank you for breakfast."

She nodded and, as they ate, didn't interrupt the silence between them. "You're having regrets about last night, aren't you?" she asked him finally.

"Are you?" he countered quickly.

Kris didn't answer him right away. "For me, last night was more than just some wonderful moments in time," she admitted reluctantly. "I realize that's not the way it was for you and I can accept that," she continued in a steady voice. "But what happened last night *won't* happen again."

Her heart was broken and he was the cause of it. The knowledge stung. Max knew he'd been too distant, and somehow that had led her to believe she'd been a one-night stand. She didn't know the truth—and he couldn't tell her.

Pain twisted him up inside. He was allowing a treasure to slip through his fingers. Yet there was nothing he could do—or more to the point—nothing he *should* do to stop her.

"Once we finish eating, we need to get going," he said brusquely.

"Where will we be heading?" she asked, her tone matching his. "I suppose the Brotherhood gave you some explicit directions."

He choked on his eggs. Composing himself quickly, then giving her a cool glance, he added, "The what?"

"I know precisely who and what you are, Max," she said calmly. "You didn't really expect to work this closely with me and not have me find out sooner or later, did you?"

He started to deny the existence of the Brotherhood, but one look at her face told him it was way too late for that. "What do you know about the Brotherhood?"

What she told him was accurate to the last detail. It shouldn't have surprised him. She knew how to gather intelligence. "How did you put all that together?"

"Following your advice," she said, then rinsed out the dishes.

"What advice?" he asked, frustrated that he had to ask for each bit of information.

"You have your secrets, I have mine. You ready to go?" she asked, turning to face him.

Her gaze was an open challenge and it took all his willpower to remain calmly seated. Along with anger there was an undeniable passion in Kris's eyes that urged him to take her in his arms. Yet, ultimately, it was the pain of betrayal he could also see on her face that kept him where he was.

"Kris, I care about you, but you want promises I can't give you," he said at last.

Her eyes blazed. "Promises? Don't flatter yourself. We both made a mistake last night. A pleasurable one, but still a mistake," she added, her body perfectly still, conveying nothing.

"What do you want from me?" he asked, wanting to make things better, but the frustration evident in his tone left the question open to another interpretation.

"I want us to finish what we set out to do," she said coldly.

She walked to the doorway, then glanced back at him. "If you ever find peace within yourself—with everything you are and could be—then come find me."

Max knew he'd never have to go find her. She was part of his heart forever. Yet the life he could offer her was the exact opposite of the one she wanted for herself—what she needed. Kris had come home wanting to find peace and a secure future. She'd know neither with him. He was a warrior. That's all he'd ever be.

THEY WERE IN THE CAR a short time later. As Kris glanced over at him, she noticed that his hands were gripping the wheel so tightly his knuckles were white. She wanted to bridge the gap between them that grew wider with each passing second, but she wasn't sure how to do that—or even if it could be done.

"We need to pick up something before we leave the area. It should have been left for us at the end of this road." Moments later he pulled up next to the mailbox and retrieved a small leather pouch that had been fastened beneath it, out of sight.

"What's that?" she asked as he got back into the SUV.

"It's just what we need to keep Mr. Nez from panicking when we show up. It's a special medicine bundle to give him protection against the *chindi*."

"So this will help him not be afraid of me?" she asked.

"He was never afraid of *you*. He thought he was seeing your sister—coming back as a *chindi*. This time I want you to unfasten your ponytail and stay well back. I'll approach him first. Once he sees the bundle, and realizes you aren't your sister, we'll have a better chance of getting him to talk to us."

"What does the bundle contain? I know you mentioned pollen and collected substances before, but you never said what those were. Do you mind me asking?"

He shook his head. "Collected substances can be almost anything. In this particular case they're beads made from the husks of juniper berries, flint, gall medicine made from certain powerful animals. They're tokens of power rooted in our creation stories."

He continued. "On the outside people often fear the things they can't control. But the *Diné* have ways of confronting the things that threaten them. That gives them power over their fears," he said as he drove north. Due to the early hour, the roads were almost empty.

They arrived at a farming and ranching community along the river valley just west of the town of Shiprock. The houses here were surrounded by fields already harvested, and several had horses browsing among the stubble left after the last cutting of alfalfa.

"There he is," Max said, pointing to an old green pickup about a quarter mile away. The high sides of the bed allowed firewood to be safely stacked as high as the top of the cab. The driver had just turned down a narrow fence-lined access road.

"So now what? Come up from behind and flag him down?" she asked. "This road's a dead end."

He considered it. "No. Let's just follow along at a distance for a bit."

They watched him pull into the home's driveway, and shortly thereafter, a woman came out the front door to greet him. She pointed to the side of the house where there was a covered porch and a metal frame containing a few logs, then went back inside.

The man backed up close to the porch, let down the tailgate of his truck, then began unloading the wood onto the ground.

"Okay, I've got an idea," Max said, reaching under the seat and bringing out a Washington Redskins cap. "Stay in the car. I'll go join him and offer to help stack the firewood."

Her hair was already loose around her shoulders as she reached for a pair of sunglasses in her purse. "This is in case he sees me. With my hair down and these sunglasses I won't look anything like my sister."

"Good thinking. Your sister's eyes and yours are almost the same shade of gold."

They parked at the end of the driveway, blocking any escape by vehicle, then Max put on the cap and climbed out his side. "Remember, stay here, inside the vehicle. I'll be back."

Kris watched him walk toward the man unloading the split logs. Now Max was in his element. His shoulders thrown back, confidence marked his steps, power in every stride. She sighed softly. Her feelings for Max were real, but she wouldn't give herself to a man who would always keep her at arm's length emotionally.

She'd complete the job she'd undertaken on her sister's behalf, then move on—just as soon as she could convince her heart to let go....

MAX APPROACHED SLOWLY, then as Charlie Nez turned to look at him, smiled. "*Yáat'ééh,* uncle. Can I give you a hand with that? You keep unloading the truck, and I'll stack the wood."

"*Ahéhee,* nephew," he replied, thanking him with a nod.

For several minutes Max and Charlie worked in silence. "I've brought you a gift," Max said after a few minutes, pausing to take a break. "Last time we met, you were worried about the you-know-what. But with this *jish* you'll never have to worry about evil spirits again. You'll be protected. It was prepared by a *hataalii* called *Hastiin Bigodii.*"

Charlie gave Max a surprised look. "He's a very powerful *hataalii,* nephew. This is a very good gift you give me."

"I need your help, uncle—the *tribe* needs your help. Will you tell me what you remember abut the day you found the dead woman? That *jish* will keep you safe, and I won't call her *chindi* by saying her name."

Max saw Charlie squinting, trying to get a closer look at Kris, who'd remained seated in the car.

"She's the sister of that dead Anglo woman. She's helping the tribe get back some property that her sister hid earlier that day for safekeeping before she died. But nobody can find it now and we need it back."

"A white woman entrusted with Navajo property?" he asked, surprised.

Max nodded. "It was necessary at the time. And I was with her before, at least until I was shot by the same man. He betrayed us." Max lifted his shirt and showed him the reddened tissue that would eventually turn into scars, souvenirs left by Harris's bullets.

Charlie looked impressed. "*Hastiin Bigodii* is known to me. I'll tell you what I know."

Max wondered if somehow Charlie Nez had realized that he was a member of the Brotherhood. "Thank you, uncle."

With a faraway look in his eyes, the old man spoke slowly, measuring his words. "I was gathering firewood to split and sell. It's how some of my relatives and I pay for our groceries. I was hurrying, because it was about to rain, and I didn't want to get stuck and have to unload the wood to dig out. At first I thought what I heard was thunder, but then I realized it was definitely gunshots from farther down the road. I tossed the last piece of wood into the truck, then got in. Once I was sure the shooting was over, and I heard a vehicle racing away, I drove back down the road. Before long I saw another car and noticed a blood trail leading up to some rocks," he said, then lapsed into a long silence.

Now that all the wood had been tossed onto the ground from the truck, Max worked alongside Charlie, stacking the wood on the porch. Although Charlie's silence stretched out, Max didn't interrupt the quiet between them. Finally the old man continued.

"The car seat on the driver's side was covered in blood, some dried, some really fresh, so I followed the trail, knowing someone was injured. That's when I found the woman. She was lying there dead beside a big slab of sandstone." He sighed deeply and then continued. "She'd written a message on the rock in her own blood. Her finger was still wet and resting on it when I came up. Then lightning struck close by and I knew that between that and the *chindi* I was in danger. I ran back to my truck, and just as I drove off, it started to rain really hard."

Another lengthy silence followed, then Charlie continued. "I would have kept right on going to the *hataalii*, too, but I needed to buy gas and supplies before heading to Arizona. While I was at the store, I got to talking to the boy working there, and he told me I'd better call the police." Their eyes met briefly. "And he was right. Her relatives deserved to know where she was before the coyotes and vultures got to her. So I made the call, then drove all the way to Tuba City to see a medicine man who has helped my family before."

Max helped him stack the rest of the firewood, but the old man never said anything more. Finally, Max asked him the one question that had been burning inside his head.

"*What* did you see written on the sandstone, uncle?" Since it had rained afterward, the only place that message existed now was in Charlie Nez's head.

"Badge," he said. "That's all it said."

Thanking him, Max returned to the truck and repeated the conversation to Kris as he drove away.

"I don't get it," she said. "Was she referring to the badge Harris had worn at one time? But both of you knew that Harris was a traitor already, so why bother to leave that message?"

"Maybe it was meant for the police," he suggested. "She didn't know if I would be alive to tell them."

"That could explain why she also wrote 'remember,'" Kris said, nodding slowly. "Did the police report mention anything about the message my sister left on the rock?"

"No. Just that there was a lot of blood on and around her body. I saw the photos, and there was no indication of her trying to write anything at all."

Kris wiped the tears from her eyes, but said nothing.

"Are you okay?" he asked softly.

She nodded, then taking a deep breath, spoke in a quiet, but unsteady voice. "It just doesn't make any sense to me. If she wanted to implicate Harris, why not write his name on that rock? Why 'badge'?"

"Obviously we're missing something here," he said after a pause.

"The only thing that's clear to me is that my sister tried to use her last minutes of life to leave us a clue. I'm not going to rest until we figure out what she meant."

Max reached for her hand but she pulled away. "No. I don't need sympathy. I need to stay in control and that'll just make it worse. We've got to stay on track."

"Agreed," he said, then after a pause, added, "I need to talk to the tribe."

"Why don't you say what you really mean—that you need to contact the Brotherhood?" she asked wearily.

"If I did, would that make you happy?"

"It would mean that you're willing to trust me," she answered quietly. "I think I deserve that much from you."

"You saved my life and I saved yours. Trust goes along with it as well."

"Yet you still hesitate around me," Kris said, holding his gaze. "And without trust, we have nothing."

Her words, vibrating with passion and conviction, touched him deeply. He'd always had a reputation for being unapproachable—a loner who needed no one. Yet Kris had shown him a side of himself he hadn't known existed. He needed her in his life. She completed him in a way nothing or no one ever had before.

"Yes, I'm part of the Brotherhood," he admitted at last. "But you can't ever tell anyone what I've just told you, or even mention the Brotherhood in connection to me. Do you understand?"

"Thank you for showing faith in me," she said in a whisper. "It means a lot to me."

"I've always trusted you, Kris. It's *me* you shouldn't trust. Your needs and mine…are poles apart."

"Maybe on the surface," she started, but then Max's cell phone rang.

He spoke hurriedly, and after several minutes placed the phone back in his pocket. "An agreement has been reached between the tribe and the sheriff's department. Detective Lassiter is now in charge of the case. He'll exchange information with us and also verify what Charlie Nez told us. When we see him we can also ask him if he knows anything about the message your sister wrote on the rock face."

"But Lassiter doesn't trust you," she said. "Would it be better for me to deal with him?"

"No. Detective Lassiter doesn't trust me, that's true enough, but he's been ordered to meet with us. He'll play ball. Feel free to jump in anytime, though."

Max called the sheriff's station next and spoke to Lassiter directly. "We need to keep our meeting private for security reasons," Max insisted. "That means away from the station."

"There's a truck stop diner called the Terminal Café on east Main in Farmington not far from the municipal buildings. You'll be as safe there as any place I can think of."

"Sounds good to me."

"By the way, Tina Reynolds's personal effects can now be released. I'll bring them over and Ms. Reynolds can sign for them."

"That's fine," Max said. "See you in fifteen then?"

"You've got it."

Max hung up and filled her in.

"Maybe we'll find a clue in my sister's personal effects," she said in a sad, tired voice. "But I've got to say I'm very surprised that Lassiter was so willing to meet with you. I expected less cooperation."

"You underestimated the clout a request from the tribal president carries," he said, then added, "But to be honest, I have a gut feeling something else has happened, and Lassiter's discovered he needs outside help."

"That's a good thing. It'll make for balance between him and us," she said, remembering what he'd taught her about the Navajo Way.

"Your words prove what I already knew. We're part of each other now."

The unexpected declaration took her breath away. By the time she'd gathered her wits, they'd reached the highway, and were heading toward the eastern border of the Navajo Nation.

Chapter Seventeen

"Watch yourself at the Terminal Café. I'll back you up if you need it, but be careful." Before she could protest, he added, "I worry. It comes with caring." Seeing the surprised look on her face, he added. "You mean a lot to me, Kris. Don't you know that? That's why this case is even more dangerous for both of us now."

Kris didn't look directly at him, afraid he'd read too much in her eyes. Max *cared*. But she'd wanted so much more from him than that. She took a steadying breath and tried to think of how Tina would have handled the situation. "We shared a special time together, but my judgment's intact. If you make a dumb move, I'll be there to point it out."

He blinked. "For a moment you sounded just like your sister."

"She's not the only tough cookie in our family. Now concentrate on what we have to do," she ordered. "What do you know about the Terminal Café?"

"I've never been there before, so we'll play it by ear."

His refusal to make plans irked her, but she didn't say anything. One battle at a time.

"Watch Lassiter," he said. "If we get there first, I want to see him arrive. I need to make sure he's not planning any surprises for us."

"You think he's setting us up, planning on arresting us for some trumped-up charge?"

"I'm not sure what he's doing, and that's what bothering me."

The drive from Shiprock didn't take long, and they entered the diner about thirty minutes later. Max chose a table near a window with a clear view of the parking area outside. "Here he comes now," he said after they'd ordered coffee.

Detective Lassiter strode in moments later. Kris watched him carefully. If anything, the man looked worn out. Spotting them, he came over, his footsteps slow and heavy.

"You look like someone who hasn't slept in a week," Max said.

"We've got a few problems at the station—and with this case." He placed the small padded manila envelope with Tina Reynolds's personal effects down on the table. "Everything else is still in the evidence room, but this was what we found on her person. There's a wallet with photos and her wristwatch."

Kris nodded, unable to get any words past the lump in her throat. She signed the paper he gave her quickly, then put the bundle on her lap.

"So, we're here to trade information," Lassiter said, focusing on Max. "What have you got for me?"

Max briefed him on what they'd learned from Charlie Nez. "But I don't remember hearing anything from the police about a message scrawled on a rock," he said, finishing.

"We never saw it," Lassiter admitted after a pause. "It *did* rain that day, pretty hard—one of the reasons why we never got clear footprints, or tire tread impressions." He sat back and rubbed his chin. "But here's the thing. We've suspected all along that Harris must have had a partner—considering the transportation issue, for one thing. And if you're right and Talbot's the man, then that explains a lot of other things."

"Like what?" Max probed.

"We began to suspect that Harris had a contact with access to the department after I found a bug under my desk. The device had come from *our* department. When pressed, the deputy in charge of tech support admitted he'd been missing one for some time. We figured Harris was behind the original theft, but we also knew Harris must have had someone else plant it," he said. "No way he could have come into the department and not be noticed," he said. "We never considered Talbot, but, thinking back, he's the perfect candidate. He was with us constantly for days following the initial crime, and had plenty of opportunity."

"Unfortunately, we haven't got anything solid on him," Max said. "But once you start looking in that direction, there's no telling what you'll find."

"Only *one* bug was planted? You sure about that?" Kris asked, composed once again. "That doesn't sound right."

"We searched the station up and down and sideways and found nothing. We even got an FBI tech from Albuquerque to sweep the station. Believe me, had there been a second bug we would have spotted it."

Max gave Kris an approving nod, then looking back at Lassiter, added, "I guess we're finished here." He placed several bills on the table, and stood. "You know how to contact the tribe, and here's my cell number if you need me." He wrote the number on a napkin, which Lassiter then put into his pocket. "If we find anything else, we'll let you know through the proper channels."

"Good luck, you two," Lassiter said.

As soon as they were in the car, Max glanced at Kris. "What made you suspect more than one bug had been planted, particularly when only one had shown up as missing?"

"I remembered a conversation about tradecraft I had with a CIA guy once. He told me bugs are sometimes planted in pairs—one that the mark can find easily enough, and the one that's meant to stay there awhile. But I suppose it's possible that Harris only had the one he ripped off." She opened the bag with Tina's effects, verified the contents, then closed it back up. She wasn't ready for more. As sadness settled over her, she lapsed into a long silence.

She didn't speak again until they hit the highway. "We've picked up a tail."

He studied the car in the distance through his rearview mirror. "Harris?"

"I don't know, but if it is him, Harris must have also planted a GPS in Lassiter's car. There are a lot of those low-tech devices out there these days, like the ones parents use to keep track of their kids."

He pressed down on the accelerator but the SUV responded sluggishly, and the engine started to miss. "We've got trouble," he said, cursing. "Whoever it was must have messed with the engine or the fuel line. I thought we were safe in a parking lot filled with cars."

"Since they didn't do anything overt, they must have wanted us away from the Café before they sprung their trap." Kris saw the black, older model luxury sedan narrowing the distance between them. "We can't outrun them, but we've got to find a better place to make a stand."

"I'll turn right at the next street," he said quickly.

They were soon in an industrial area with several abandoned brick buildings and a big metal warehouse. There, the chances were less that innocent civilians would be caught up in a gun battle. He made another turn without signaling or touching the brakes, and the tires squealed in protest, but the SUV, lower and more stable than most, took the maneuver well.

"There are two of them back there now," Kris said. "There's a pickup behind the sedan."

"I'm going to cut up that alley," he said, gesturing.

He made another hard right, taking them up a narrow alley with another big warehouse and a double loading dock. It looked closed, and nobody was around. The road was a dead end. "My bad. I was hoping we could circle around, but it looks like we'll have to make our stand here."

Max hit the brakes and swung the wheel around, attempting to slide around in a moonshiner's turn. The car was sputtering, barely running now.

Suddenly the engine backfired loudly, then died. They lurched forward a few feet, then came to a stop sideways, the driver's side facing the oncoming car.

"Get out! I'll cover you," Max said, pulling his gun.

Kris jumped out the passenger's side and, using the hood for protection and to steady her aim, called out to him. "Your turn. I'll cover you."

She fired at the driver, who ducked as she squeezed off the shot, but continued straight toward them.

Max was just coming out of the SUV when the big black car slammed into the driver's door. The impact hurled him to the pavement alongside Kris, who'd also been thrown to the ground by the force of the collision.

He made it to his knees just as a round object struck the pavement beside them.

"Grenade!" she yelled, making a desperate grab for the plastic device.

Max turned just as it exploded. There was a loud pop and fragments stung his skin. Instantly, his eyes began to burn and he started to cough. "Tear gas!" he managed.

Fighting the urge to tug at their burning skin and eyes, they tried to make a run for it. Neither made it more than few feet because of the coughing spasms that wracked their bodies. Max staggered, heard a noise behind him and raised his arm, but it was too late. He took a shot across his head with a leather sap and everything went black.

MAX WOKE UP SLOWLY and found himself handcuffed and his legs tied with what looked like clothesline. Kris, who like him was tied to a metal bracket at the rear of the van, had one side of her handcuffs free and was wiping the tear gas residue off her face and neck with a wet towel. Talbot was driving, and

Harris was on the passenger side watching her, his pistol aimed and ready.

"She'll wipe you off next, Natoni, so hang on for a minute."

His skin still felt as if it were on fire. "We'll need more than water," he managed to say.

"I brought mineral oil and alcohol. The mineral oil will help protect your skin, and the alcohol will replace the burning with a cooling sensation. But for the record, I couldn't care less if you scratch your skin bloody. The only reason I'm helping you is because you're of no use to me until you can think straight again," he said, then added, "And I sure as heck don't want to get any on me."

"How kind," Kris drawled as she started to wipe the residue off Max's face.

"You're alive. I've met my quota of kindness today." Harris spat out. "Now, if you want to keep breathing, you're going to have to figure out where Tina hid that platinum. I'm tired of going around in circles with this."

The van pulled to a stop on a gravel road, and Talbot climbed out. A few seconds later, he opened the two rear doors. "Out."

"I'm tied to the van, Einstein," Max snapped.

Harris grabbed Kris and pressed the gun to her head. "Cut the rope holding him to the van," he told Talbot, "then his feet." Looking at Max, Harris added, "If you try anything, she'll go first."

After the clothesline that bound his feet together was cut, Max swung his legs over to climb out. Kris suddenly slapped away Harris's gun and head-butted him.

Max grabbed Talbot with his legs in a scissor's lock, pulling them both to the ground. But Talbot broke free and tasered him. In agony, Max couldn't move.

Harris pulled back out of Kris's one-handed reach, gun still in his hand. He came around to the rear of the van, and seeing that Max was covered, reached in and cracked Kris hard on the knee with the barrel of his weapon.

She gasped but didn't scream.

"Try hitting me again, sweetheart, and I'll pistol-whip that pretty face of yours. Now stay still and behave," Harris said. He stuck his pistol into his belt at the small of his back. Then, taking the knife from Talbot, he cut her other hand free from the bracket in the van, and yanked her roughly out onto the ground beside Max.

"Here's the deal," he said, looking at Kris. "I'm betting you're the key. Natoni has had more than enough time to tell the tribe where to find the stuff, and if he hasn't figured it out by now, that leaves *you*. I've done some homework and I know that you and your sister were close."

"Doesn't matter. I still don't know where it is," she said firmly. "If I did, we'd have picked it up by now and every officer in the state would be looking for you," she said, glancing at Max who was starting to come around.

"I still think *you* can figure it out. All you need is a little more incentive to come up with the answer. 'Remember,' as the note said." Harris handed Talbot his knife, and the tall, slender man stepped over behind Max, yanking his head back by the hair, and brought the knife blade down by his throat.

"Maybe I should start with a less vulnerable spot—save the throat for last," Talbot said, moving the blade around in front of Max's face now. "We can start by taking things away…like his eye. Which one of your boyfriend's eyes would you prefer to see on the end of my blade, sweet thing, the right or left one?"

She stared at him, but was unable to speak.

"No preference?" Talbot pressed the point of his knife against the skin beneath Max's right eye until a drop of blood appeared.

"Wait," she said, looking around. From the landmarks she could approximate where they were. "Lassiter just returned my sister's personal effects. As I was looking through the photos, I remembered our first camping trip together," she said, coming up with the most plausible story she could invent off-the-cuff. "Our mom was still alive then, and we went to an area around the Four Corners, not too far from here, I think. There's a good chance the platinum may be hidden where we spent that night."

She paused for dramatic effect before continuing. "But I was ten years old and I wasn't exactly driving at the time. All I can tell you is that from our camp site we could see Ute Mountain and Ship Rock, but it was from the north, you know, not the west view that most people photograph. It was among the piñon trees, because we looked for nuts. And there was a trading post nearby where we stopped for gas. It was off on a dirt road, not next to the highway. I *would* recognize the area if I saw it again."

Harris gave her a long speculative look, then finally nodded to Talbot, who released Max, then closed the blade on his knife. "Too bad, Natoni. I was looking forward to a little fun."

"Brutality always seems to entertain little minds," Kris said, looking directly at him.

"Why don't *you* entertain me, then, witch?" Talbot came toward her, opening the knife blade.

"Not now. We need her alive," Harris snapped.

"But we don't need him," Talbot said, glancing back at Max as he brought a pistol from his jacket pocket.

"Not on the treasure hunt, no. He'd only be an extra complication. But we need him here as…incentive."

"This wasn't part of the plan," Talbot said.

"I've seen the way these two look at each other, and I've decided on a much more interesting method to insure Ms. Reynolds remains cooperative. Ever construct a fire bomb, Talbot?"

Talbot shook his head.

"Well, you're about to," Harris said with a slow smile. "And this one will be attached to Natoni—up close and personal."

He turned to look at Kris. "If you're messing with us, sweetheart, all I'll have to do is call the number of the cell phone we're going to attach to that bomb—and boom. The spark will reduce Natoni to ashes."

"Don't worry about me," Max told Kris. "I doubt these two can find their butts with both hands, much less make any kind of bomb."

"Oh really?" Harris's smile was lethal. "We'll just have to see about that."

Turning Kris over to Talbot, Harris took the taser and shot Max for a second time.

While he was incapacitated, Harris taped his legs together tightly, so he'd be unable to walk, much less run.

Then, making sure she could see him work, Harris brought out a red plastic gasoline container. Using the punch from a multi-tool combination knife, he punched a hole in its side just below the level of the fluid inside, then twisted it a few times to enlarge the opening. A small amount of gasoline leaked out, adding the acrid smell to the air.

"No smoking," he warned, then chuckled. Next he brought out a cheap cell phone and taped it to the side of the gasoline container right above the leak with a few laps of duct tape. He then taped the handle of the container to the loop of Max's belt, in the back so it couldn't be reached easily.

Harris stood back to survey his work. "Folks, I don't know how much power this has, but remember the caution signs around gas stations warning people not to use their cell phones or PDAs? Sparks and gasoline vapors do *not* mix, and things will only get worse if Max struggles, spilling gas on himself. If I call this number, the cell phone will turn on, maybe spark just a little—and surprise, instant Zozobra. You guys *do* know about that tradition—burning up Old Man Gloom before Fiesta de Santa Fe?"

"You can't do this," Kris said urgently. "Sparks can come from your clothes in this dry climate. He could die even if you *don't* make the call."

"Hey, it's a chance I'm willing to take," Harris replied. "If you don't find the platinum for us in, say, two hours, then the call will go through for sure."

"That's not long enough. You've got to give me more time," Kris argued, looking around at the terrain. "I'm not exactly sure where we are, except northwest of Shiprock. We're in the right general area, I think, but I don't remember specifics, like which road to take. It might be an hour or more before I find it. The area's changed since I was a kid."

"The Arizona state line is less than an hour from here, and the place you're talking about has to be closer than that, but hey, okay. Two-and-a-half hours. And, if we're getting close and you're really cooperative, maybe another fifteen minutes. But if it looks like you're jerking us around…"

"If *anything* happens to him, I won't cooperate with you," Kris said. "Count on it."

"I think you will—*after* we have a little fun with you," Harris said, giving her a slow, lecherous look.

She didn't have to ask what kind of fun he meant, and with Talbot there too… "Let me say goodbye to Max first."

"How touching. Okay, but make it fast," Harris said. "And try not to shock him."

Kris went to Max's side, then leaned over as if to give him a kiss, and whispered, "I'm buying you time, that's all." Drawing back, she slipped off the chain with the four leaf clover Tina and given her and placed it around his neck.

"For luck," she added, then walked away.

Max watched her leave, knowing her fears and wishing he could have told her that he expected to be out of the cuffs as soon as they left. It was all a matter of skill and the right touch.

Chapter Eighteen

Despite Max's best intentions, an unexpected snag put a crimp in his plans. All he'd needed was a small piece of wire, or the equivalent of that—something sturdy enough to help him pick the locking mechanism.

Sitting on a dirt road somewhere in the general area of Beclabito, New Mexico, though, the pickings were slim. He turned around slowly, searching his surroundings. There was an arroyo not far from where he was, and something was sticking up—a metal beam that was part of a flood control barrier—a combination of steel and *wire*.

Studying the ground by his feet, he spotted a large chunk of quartzite and began to move his legs against the sharp edge. As the motion caused the gasoline container to slosh, he felt the cool touch of gasoline on his skin. But there was no choice, he had to walk and cutting the tape was the first thing on his agenda.

Five minutes later, he was free of the tape. Two minutes after he'd twisted off a piece of wire from the barrier, he was free of the cuffs. Both hands loose now, he pulled off the tape and removed the cell phone. Setting it on the ground, closed and upwind to keep it away from gasoline vapors, he unfastened the gasoline container from his belt and stepped away. His shirt was still soaked, so he took it off and placed it beside the gasoline.

Now, with the same phone Talbot and Harris had meant to use as a tool to destroy him, he'd get the Brotherhood's help. Grabbing the cell phone and moving even farther away, he tried to make a call but the phone's battery was too low. Even if Talbot had called in, there would have probably been no sparks produced at all. That was the ultimate irony.

He looked around. There were no dwellings or vehicles within sight and, though he recognized the general area, he wasn't sure which direction he should run to find help quickly. From the time frame Kris had given Harris, he was almost sure he knew where she was going. She was taking him to the vicinity of the gas station where they'd gone to talk to the attendant. But she'd then have to choose a road in the area. Would she go west or east of the station—north or south of the highway? He could be off by miles and there was no room for error, not when her life was at stake. He had to pinpoint her exact location and do that quickly.

The realization that he was out of options, miles from transportation, made it harder to stay focused. The need to save the woman who'd come to mean the world to him was taking control of his every thought. If anything happened to her on his watch…. He forced that fear aside.

Taking a deep breath, Max turned in a slow circle, checking the distant landmarks and trying to decide which direction to go. As he did, he felt the gold charm she'd given him burn into his chest. Driven by something he couldn't understand, he reached for the *jish* still attached to his belt. He could feel it calling to him, promising without words, and whispering of a way to save her.

There were no stars out now, except the setting sun, but that was a star, too. Knowing he had to try for her sake, Max slipped the gold charm necklace she'd given him off his neck, then opened the *jish* and brought out the crystal. Holding both in one hand, he applied the pollen mixture to his eyes, then allowed the sun to bathe the rock crystal in brightness.

As his Song filled the air, everything around him stilled. He waited, staring intently at the crystal, but nothing happened. Max pushed back his frustration, taking another deep breath, and concentrated only on Kris.

Seconds stretched out and, slowly, he felt the power building inside him, beginning in his heart then spreading outward. He opened himself to those feelings and a vision began to form in his mind's eye. He saw Kris walking around, stumbling, then being yanked to her feet by Harris.

Minutes passed as he watched the scene unfold. When the vision finally ended, he drew in an unsteady breath. There was no denying it now. As the *hataalii* had promised, the gift of stargazing was his. Love had been the key.

Against all odds, he'd found her. He knew which road she was on now—just east of Beclabito, and north of the highway. His best chance of freeing her would be to ambush Harris and Talbot. But he was unarmed and, most important of all, he had no way of getting there quickly enough to make a difference.

Out of options, Max put his shirt back on, then began running, but now he knew which direction to go. He'd only gone a quarter of a mile when he saw half a dozen horses grazing. A young Navajo man in his late teens was watching the animals from the shade of a piñon tree, munching on an apple.

Max came up slowly so the boy could see him approach. "Nephew, my clan is Living Arrow, and I was born for Bitter Water," he said, naming his mother's clan first and his father's clan last, according to their custom.

The boy nodded and answered, "I'm of the Salt People, born for Bitter Water."

"Then we're related," Max said. "Although we've never met, I need a favor from you. I work for the tribe and am trying to stop some criminals. I need you to loan me one of your horses, and then go get some backup for me as fast as you can."

"Uncle, these horses are under my care. I can't give you one unless I go with you."

Max didn't blame him. In the boy's shoes, he wouldn't have done it any differently. "All right. You can ride with me part way. Once I verify where our tribe's enemies are, I'll need you to ride back as fast as the wind and take a message to *Hastiin Bigodii*. You may already know him. He belongs to the Salt People Clan, too. Will you do this for me?"

The boy nodded. "My father knows the *hataalii*. I'll help you. We'll take my two fastest horses." He whistled and a pinto came over, followed by a brown chestnut. Both had halters on them. The boy handed Max a length of rope to use in lieu of reins.

"Do you have any kind of weapon?" Max asked, wishing he still had his own pistol.

The boy shrugged. "Just a pocket knife. Usually a few rocks or a big stick is enough to keep the coyotes and wild dogs away. You can borrow it, I guess."

"Thanks. You'll get it back," Max said, taking the tool. "Now let's ride." He mounted the horse in one smooth, effortless move.

They raced along the slopes of the rising low foothills, around rock formations, and up the narrow draws, slowing down only when the terrain forced them to do so. Traveling over ground no wheeled vehicles could cross, they made good time.

The moon was over their shoulders by the time they spotted the lights of a slow-moving vehicle off to their right.

Max brought his horse to a stop and stared down into a narrow canyon at the faint outline of the van traveling along the dirt road. The vehicle had stopped, although the lights were still on. In the glare of the headlights, he could see a figure looking around the base of a refrigerator-sized boulder close to the road. Judging from his size and shape, it was most likely Harris.

Max looked at the boy, who'd come up beside him. "Where does this road lead?"

"From the highway it leads north to a corral and hay barn

where my neighbor winters his animals. There's a stock tank and windmill there, too, so they always have water."

"Is that where the road ends?"

The boy nodded. "To go any farther, you'd have to travel on foot or on horseback."

Max dismounted and turned his horse back over to the boy. Keeping the animal with him now would only increase his chances of being seen and caught. He'd have to move as silently as Moon traveling across the skies.

"Go and contact *Hastiin Bigodii*. Tell him Thunder sent you. And, nephew, ride like someone's life depends on it— because it does."

As the boy galloped away, Max ran along the top of the mesa. He circled toward a spot around a steep curve where the road cut between two tall bluffs—a narrow pass that was vulnerable. A rockslide at just the right place would effectively impede the passage of any vehicle back to the highway.

Picking his way down around boulders that came up to his waist, he stopped halfway down the steep slope. Finding a large rock that looked vulnerable, he put his foot against it and pushed as hard as he could. It wobbled and slipped downslope a few inches.

Trying once more, he managed to topple the rock completely, sending it crashing downhill. Like balls on a pool table, the first rock smashed into others, knocking them loose and sending them on collision courses with others down the slope. A few seconds later, the cloud of dust lifted and he could see that a dozen or more rocks and boulders, most of them at least the size of watermelons, had tumbled down onto the road.

Repeating the process a few feet farther across the slope, he managed to send several more big boulders down onto the road. It would take at least fifteen minutes to clear the road and, since it was getting dark, that promised to make the job even harder. They'd have to work hard and it would take both men to roll the rocks out of the way in order to get back to civilization. Harris probably wouldn't let Kris help because they'd have to untie her hands and feet to do that. Once freed, they wouldn't be able to guarantee that Kris wouldn't run away or try and disarm one of them.

Max took a position behind the area where the van would have to come to a stop and crouched low behind a boulder. Five minutes passed, and while he waited, he looked over the terrain, mapping out a future escape route and possible hiding places.

Finally he heard a vehicle approaching. Even in the moonlight he could tell it was Harris and Talbot's van. Ducking low, he waited and listened. Suddenly there was the sound of sliding tires and a loud curse.

Talbot climbed out of the driver's side, followed by Harris. While the men were distracted, Max crept up quickly. Using the van itself to screen his movements from the pair, he picked the lock that held the back doors shut and pulled them open.

The relief mirrored on Kris's face as she saw him wound through him and squeezed. He had to force himself not to pull her into his arms. Signaling her to remain still, he cut the cord that held her tied to a bracket on the wall of the van. Although still cuffed, her hands weren't bound behind her back, and she'd now have enough mobility to defend herself. Getting her out of those cuffs would have to wait until they had more time.

When Max reached in to help her out, she edged away long enough to grab Talbot's jacket, which was resting over the backrest of the front seat. Seconds later, they were climbing the bluff and heading north, hoping to throw off pursuit by moving in the opposite direction of the highway. They were already high above a rock shelf that circled the mesa, out of view of the van, when they both heard Harris shout.

"Come back, Reynolds, or Natoni is dead."

"Keep going up and to your left," Max urged. "We have to find a place where they won't be able to circle around and spot us from the van. Once we lose them, we'll hide out until help arrives—which shouldn't be long," he added with an encouraging smile.

Kris kept up with him, staying close so they could whisper back and forth. "Are you armed? How did you find me? Do you have a car nearby?"

"Just a pocket knife, I'll tell you how I found you later, and no car. Save your energy for the climb and try not to knock loose any rocks that'll give away our position. And keep a look out for rattlers, too. It's not too late in the year for them to be out hunting for rodents."

"They can't bite through a boot, can they?"

"Not likely. Just be careful where you put your hands when you have to steady yourself. And keep moving."

They were near the top when Max signaled her to stop. He looked at the rock shelf that formed one of the hardest layers of sandstone on the big cliff. A large section had separated slightly from the main formation and created a narrow slit—a vertical cave parallel to the cliff face.

"I'll go in first," he whispered, "but I don't expect any problems since cobwebs still lay across the opening."

Max turned sideways, feeling with his toe, and inched into the opening. Three feet farther he realized the small cavern was larger than he'd expected. It wasn't much more than a vertical crack in the mesa, but they had enough room to sit down on the rock floor. Above the top of the rock wall he could see stars, which meant the air would stay fresh, too.

"It's like a stone hallway leading nowhere," he said.

"Good hiding place," she answered.

"We'll stay in here for a while, if you're ready for a break," he said, then removed her cuffs with the same piece of wire he'd used for his own. "Though help is on the way, it probably won't arrive anytime soon," he added, telling her about the boy.

She reached into Talbot's jacket and handed him the cell phone. "This is why I took the jacket. I don't know if it'll work from here, but give it a shot."

Getting no signal from inside the cave, he stepped outside and maneuvered along the ledge of the cliff. Finally he managed to get his contact in the Brotherhood. Yet the connection kept breaking every few seconds. Realizing it was the connection, not the battery, Max continued to call back, leaving more bits of his message each time.

Finally he returned to the cave. He was still unsure how much of his message had gone through, but he needed to save the battery for a time when he could get a better signal.

Max explained what had happened, adding, "I also tried to send a text message, but we'll have to wait and see if they received enough of it to nail down our location. If they did, we can expect backup and an extraction team soon."

"We should get back on the move and try new locations with the cell phone," she suggested. "Sometimes just a few yards can make a difference."

He shook his head. "With Talbot and Harris close by, armed and gunning for us, this is the safest place for us right now."

"You're right. The oldest rule of warfare is control the high ground."

They sat with their backs against the sandstone wall so they could see the opening and anyone who got within a few feet of the cave. Max placed his arm over her protectively, not because she needed protection, but to reassure himself that, for now, they had each other.

Kris settled against him. "Back there, when you opened the van doors… I was never more glad to see anyone in my life," she said, sighing as he tightened his hold.

"Having them take you from me made me crazy inside," he said in a thick voice. "But it helped me realize some important things."

Kris looked at him expectantly. "Go on," she whispered.

"I've always gone out of my way to avoid being needed by anyone—or to need anyone. Then I met you, and that all changed," he said quietly. "My feelings for you go deep, Kris, but with people gunning for us, I knew that entanglements might get us both killed. That's why I've been fighting this so hard."

"Some things are just meant to be," she said quietly.

"Maybe so," he answered gently.

"How did you find me?" As she moved back so she could see his face, she noticed what she hadn't seen before. "Does it have something to do with the fact you moved your *jish* from your left to your right side?" she asked, touching the medicine pouch lightly.

Seeing her bruised knuckles, he lifted her hand to his lips. "I'm glad you got a few good punches off."

"You're avoiding my question," she answered, then in a somber tone added, "Neither one of us knows if we'll get out of this alive, Max. Let's not waste the moments we do have by hiding behind secrets."

Seeing the love reflected in her eyes, he dropped the barriers that had stood between them. They weren't necessary—not anymore.

"I never really believed I was a stargazer," he began, keeping her hand in his. "I figured—or maybe hoped is a better word—that it was just something that happened that once. But when they took you away something snapped inside me. I was ready to do whatever I had to do to find you. That's when I felt the power of the *jish*. It was calling to me, like a voice at the back of my mind that I couldn't ignore. So I brought the crystal out, pointed it to the sun, and held it next to your necklace."

"Were you just hoping, or did you somehow know that you could make it work?" she asked, her voice barely audible.

"I've always trusted the things I can see and touch, and stargazing doesn't fit that bill. But if need—the kind that rips at a man's guts—had anything to do with it, I knew I'd get answers." He held her gaze and continued. "It was a test of everything. If there was any truth to my stargazing abilities, then I knew my heart would find yours across time and space."

"I felt your mind's touch," Kris said. "It was a gentle whisper winding through my thoughts, an assurance I couldn't explain. I knew you were coming for me."

He bent down to take her mouth with his and she parted her lips, inviting him to take more. Fire coursed through his veins. He could spend a lifetime memorizing her taste, her softness and the way she sighed when she surrendered to him.

Though it was one of the most difficult things he'd ever done, Max pulled back, burying his face in her hair for one last moment before moving away. "We can't allow ourselves to get this distracted. If they find us...."

He didn't have to complete the thought. She knew death trailed them now. "No matter what happens, we'll face it together."

"Hold on to that thought." He reached for her hand, kissed it, then went to the front of the cave to keep watch.

Chapter Nineteen

"Let me spell you for a while," she murmured, joining him at the mouth of the cave after an hour had passed. They could hear Talbot and Harris below them moving around, and see the beams of light as they used flashlights to search the cliffs.

"They know we're still in this area," Max replied softly. "They just don't know where to look. But that's bound to change sooner than we'd like, especially if one of them finds our footprints and climbs up this cliff."

As Max turned to look at her, the four-leaf clover he was still wearing around his neck shimmered in the moonlight. She touched it gently, remembering Tina.

"After my sister gave me that charm, she started wearing something else," Kris said, her thoughts drifting. "I remember seeing it in the photos she'd send me from time to time. It was a…badger," she finished after a brief pause.

"That fetish was made by a Zuni friend of mine. I gave it to her because it fit her."

"Fit her, how?"

"Each fetish is said to house the spirit of the animal depicted. Powers that are associated with that particular animal are then magnified in the human that cares for it. The badger is associated with tenacity and self-confidence. The badger is also a ferocious fighter despite its small size."

"That described my sister perfectly," she agreed with a sad smile. Kris lapsed into a thoughtful silence then looked back at him. "All this time we've assumed that Tina wrote *badge* on that rock as a way of implicating Harris. But here's another thought. What if she'd really been trying to write the word *badger* and ran out of…time?" she finished, her voice breaking.

He reached for her hand, squeezed it, then focused again on the men scouring the area for them. "If you're right about that, it gives her message an entirely new slant."

"The badger fetish was *not* in her personal effects," she said, then after a shaky breath, added, "I think she was telling *you* to find the badger."

Max considered it for several long moments, then nodded. "You may be right," he said at last. "She might have figured that the connection she and I had would make it easier for me as a stargazer to track the fetish."

"I think she probably left the badger with the platinum. Find one and you'll find the other. *That's* what she was trying to tell us—remember Badger. It fits the way she thinks."

"She always said that the day I made peace with my gift it would become my best ally."

Kris started to reply when they both suddenly heard a soft yet distinctive thump at the back of the cave. It was followed by a low but unmistakably feline growl that reverberated in the confines of the cave. The scent of blood soon filled the passageway.

Max held a finger to his lips. "Mountain lion with a fresh kill," he whispered, urging her to her feet and out the cave's front opening.

Once outside, he motioned for her to walk up the slope so the mountain lion would have a harder time spotting them. They moved parallel across the side of the mesa, downwind from the cave. Once they'd put several hundred yards between themselves and the cougar, Max led her gradually downhill so they were less likely to be silhouetted against the skyline.

At long last he spoke. "The fact that the cat had a fresh kill made it even more dangerous. We were lucky the animal came in through the top of the cave. Going past it to get out would have been impossible."

She nodded pensively. "Where are we headed now, besides away from the cougar?"

"We're even farther from the highway than before, but if we can work our way south, we may be able to meet up with the Brotherhood warriors. I'm hoping they aren't too far from our location now."

"But if we get too close to the road, we'll get picked off by Harris and Talbot. Now that we do have information they want, they're the last people I want to run into." She continued in a barely audible voice. "I'd like to think I'd die before I'd reveal anything to those two, but I've spoken to marines who've been tortured."

"They won't catch us," he assured in a firm tone. "Out here—this is my turf. I know how to stay alive." He led her through a tangle of rocks and shrubbery, then, hearing a shot ring out in the distance, stopped and looked around.

"If they spotted the mountain lion in that cave, then they probably have a thermal imager," he said. "I remember seeing some kind of camera-like gadget on the floor of the passenger side. Maybe that's what it was."

"If they were able to detect the cougar through its heat signature, we've lost the advantage the darkness gives us. I know how hard it is to counter those devices," she said. "If they can angle in on whatever hiding place we choose, they'll see us like it was the middle of the afternoon. Our only chance is to put more physical barriers between us, so keep moving."

Spotting a blur of motion ahead, Kris focused on it. A second or two later, she saw the mountain lion leap onto a rock below them, then go into the brush, uninjured. He raced over the ridge and disappeared from view. She breathed a silent sigh of relief, glad he was safe.

"Maybe we can circle them, staying behind the rocks," she suggested. "If the cat got away, so can we."

"I have another idea," Max said. "According to the boy who lent me the horse, this road leads to a place where a Navajo family winters their livestock. Harris and Talbot are forcing us to move in that direction anyway, so let's use it to our advantage. We can hide our heat signatures by getting into the stock tank and keeping only our noses above the water."

"I saw the place briefly while I was leading them around, stalling for time. But Harris will also think of that possibility and return to check it out. He'll look inside the stock tank too, for sure."

"One of them will probably be keeping watch with the nightscope, which means he'll be occupied while the other comes over for a look. We'll position ourselves to strike and grab whoever it is and pull him under water the second he peers over the rim. The other one won't be able to shoot without hitting his partner."

"Okay. That's a great plan. Whoever's closest will neutralize whichever man approaches first. If it falls to me, I'll grab his gun and break his wrist," she said. "Rapid dominance is the key here. Then you can handle the second man when he comes over to help. If we can get one of their pistols that'll increase the odds in our favor, too."

Max noted that there hadn't been the slightest hesitancy in her voice. "Overconfidence can get you killed," he said quietly.

"It's not overconfidence," she said, her voice somber and sure. "I've been trained to take away a weapon, and I'm motivated and in shape. If it's Harris, I might have a rougher time of it, but I *will* win. Count on it."

Somehow, he didn't doubt her. "Okay. Let's go."

They made their way as noiselessly as possible through the thick brush, using a small arroyo to keep out of sight as long as possible.

Ten minutes later they reached the winter camp. The large

stock tank was about four feet above ground level and maybe twenty feet in diameter.

After hiding the phone where it wouldn't get wet, they rubbed out their tracks as best as they could and slipped into the tank.

"Cold!" she gasped, trying not to splash the water.

"Yeah. Just be glad it's not the dead of winter."

She nodded, shivering, then lowered herself beneath the water's surface, feeling the bottom with her shoes and trying to see how sure the footing was. She was relieved to discover that it was sandy, not mossy or slippery.

It didn't take long for Harris and Talbot to arrive. Unaware of how close they were to Max and her, Harris kept calling out instructions to his partner. Talbot, meanwhile, kept cursing, complaining about the difficulty of watching through the nightscope without stumbling.

Footsteps got closer. Kris saw Max nod slightly, then duck completely under the water. Reluctantly, she did the same, keeping her head close to the metal rim of the tank so she could look up. The minute she saw a face, she'd spring into action.

The voices sounded strange to her filtering through a layer of water, but they were still distinctive. "Give me the friggin' scope, if you're such a spaz, Talbot."

"Here, take it," Talbot answered. "What makes you so sure they'd double back and come here?"

"It's what I'd do—run in the most unlikely direction. Now make yourself useful," Harris added. "Check out the stock tank. That's the only place we wouldn't be able to spot them with the scope."

"You'd think they'd even consider going for a swim? It's in the low fifties, maybe colder. They'd be ice cubes by now."

"Check it out anyway," Harris insisted.

As Talbot leaned over the tank, Kris reached out of the water, grabbing Talbot and smashing his wrist as she pulled him over the rim of the tank.

Talbot yelped as he toppled headfirst into the water, his arms flailing for anything to grab onto. Pulling his inverted face toward her body, she kneed him as hard as possible.

Harris ran over but, forewarned, he was ready when Max popped out of the water. Moving back about a foot, he brought out his pistol.

Max dove beneath the water instantly, bumping into Talbot, who'd pulled away from Kris. Grabbing him, he felt for the pistol tucked into Talbot's belt and yanked it free.

Armed, Max burst back to the surface, several feet away from where he'd been.

Harris, flashlight in hand, was looking the other way when Max squeezed the trigger. The flashlight suddenly went dark as Harris ducked low, firing back wildly.

"Get down!" Max yelled, seeing Kris's head to his left, just above the surface.

Numb with cold, Max swam sluggishly through the water, trying to reach a new position before coming up to look for Harris. When he finally rose up, pistol ready, all he could hear were running footsteps.

Max caught a glimpse of Harris as he disappeared around the barn. "Harris is making a run for it," he yelled out to Kris. "Where's Talbot?"

Kris stood, the water coming to her breasts, and pointed to a form floating facedown on the far side of the tank. "He's either unconscious or dead," she said, making her way toward the body. "There's a lot of blood in the water."

"I'll take care of Talbot." Max gave her the handgun. "Watch out for Harris in case he comes back."

Max reached the tall, redheaded man, and turned him around so he was faceup. He knew then where at least one of Harris's errant shots had gone. There was a bullet hole in Talbot's throat, but the blood wasn't pumping out anymore, just seeping slowly. Talbot was gone.

FIVE MINUTES LATER, Max and Kris stood beside the stock tank, shivering and looking down at Talbot's body on the ground between them. The bullet had passed clear through Talbot, severing his spinal cord. He'd probably died instantly.

Hearing the roar of approaching vehicles, Max glanced at Kris. "The cavalry arrives."

"Maybe they'll go after Harris," she said.

"That's exactly what they'll do. Harris doesn't know it yet, but he would have been far better off staying here with us to face the music than trying to get away from the Brotherhood—which, remember, you don't know anything about."

"I've got you covered," she said with a nod. "About Harris…will they keep at it until they catch him?"

He nodded. "It'll be relentless, and I guarantee you that they won't ease up until he's in our hands." He took a deep breath, then let it out slowly. "But don't worry about that now. You and I have other business."

Two vehicles, a big truck and a small SUV arrived before Max could explain further. After he and Kris had been given warm blankets to cover themselves, he went to speak to the driver of the SUV.

Their conversation was quick and to the point. The men inside got out and after giving Max two dry coats, hurried to join the ones in the truck. As they drove off, Max could hear the roar of other vehicles in the area who'd also joined the search.

Max returned to where Kris stood and handed her the coat. "Here you go. It's dry and very warm," he said, adjusting his own.

"I hung back on purpose while you spoke to the men," she said. "I figured that what they'd prize most is their anonymity."

"You're right about that. Their lives depend on it."

"And what's next for us?" she asked.

"They don't need our help hunting Harris down. They want us to go after the platinum."

"Can you see it in your mind, stargazer?" she whispered.

He reached down for his *jish*, but suddenly realized it was gone. "Maybe the stock tank," he said running back toward it.

They both searched, but there was nothing there to be found. "If it's up on the bluff, or somewhere along the trail, it's long gone," he said at last, the knowledge knifing through him.

"Maybe you don't need the *jish*," she answered quietly. "Dig deep inside yourself and find the strength I know is so much a part of you. Stargazing is your gift—it's within you."

He took her hand in both of his and pressed it to his heart. "My strength with yours." As his Song filled the air, a blanket of peace enfolded them.

When his Song ended, Max stood silently, surrendering to the power that filled him as he embraced his destiny. Time ceased to matter as a vision began to unfold. He was soaring like a bird over a wooded area not far from where Tina's body had been found. As he traveled past a hollow stump, he saw the badger fetish sitting on top of it. It would have been impossible to see except from above.

He'd expected the vision to end there, but it suddenly shifted. This time everything had a fluid look to it…an ever-shifting quality that spoke of what might be. He saw Kris… and a future that had yet to transpire.

Chapter Twenty

Duty and love calling him back, Max came out of the trance.

He drew in a breath and opened his eyes. "I've got the answers we needed. I know where the platinum is. But to find the exact spot, I'll need to pay attention to the terrain, so you drive," he said, tossing her the keys.

They hurried to the SUV the Brotherhood had left for them and soon were back on the road, the heater running full blast. "Your sister trusted me even before I'd learned to trust myself."

"She believed in you—as I do," Kris answered.

Max gave her the details of what he'd seen in the first vision. "I know that place, I recognized it, but of course there's still a chance I'm way off base," he added, fastening his seat belt.

"You better hope you're not," Harris said, suddenly rising from the back of the cab and pressing the gun barrel to the back of Kris's head. "I'm getting tired of games. Take out your pistol with your left hand and hand it to me by the barrel."

"How did you get here?" Max snapped, slowly following Harris's instructions.

Harris took Max's pistol and stuck it into a pocket. "I ditched the van in an arroyo and circled back. Your pals are still searching for my wheels, I guess. As always, a little improvisation works miracles."

Max turned slightly toward him, reaching down to unfasten his seat belt, and Harris suddenly tensed up. "Keep the seat belt tight, buddy," he growled. "I won't hesitate to kill her if you even breathe wrong. I have nothing to lose now. Either I get the platinum and get away, or I'm as good as dead."

"If anything at all happens to her, you're still dead. I'll hunt you down."

"I'm not interested in you or your girlfriend," Harris said. "After I've got the platinum, if you cooperate, you'll still be alive. I'll dump you in the sticks and be gone. By the time you can report in I'll be in Arizona, or maybe Utah or Colorado. But it's your choice. Do as I say, or she dies now."

"I'll take you to it," Max said, his voice flat and emotionless.

"Don't do it," Kris said, glancing over at Max. "There's no way he's going to let us live once he has what he wants."

"I have no real reason to kill you, unless you give me one," Harris argued reasonably. "I *will* make sure you can't come after me, but that's all that needs to happen. Once the state lab figures out that the man who 'died' in my car wreck had already been buried once before, they'll know I'm still alive anyway."

Kris wanted to argue the point, but seeing Max shake his head imperceptibly, she remained silent.

As they reached the highway, the phone the Brotherhood had left for them, currently on the seat beside Max, began to ring.

"Pick it up and put it on speaker," Harris ordered.

Max did as he asked, then heard *Hastiin Bigodii*'s voice. "Harris double-backed, so be on your guard," he said, unaware that his warning had come too late.

Glancing in the rearview mirror, Kris saw that Harris was completely focused on Max, and on the call. His gun hand had dropped slightly so the barrel was no longer in line with her head but, rather, with the edge of the seat.

Kris slammed hard on the brakes and, as she'd expected, she and Max were jerked hard, but Harris wasn't wearing a seat belt. He flew forward between the split seat backs and bumped his head on the gear shift. The gun went off with a deafening pop and Max felt the impact of a bullet into the metal floorboard by his left foot.

Max bent back Harris's hand, trying to pry the gun away from him. Kris reacted at nearly the same instant, grabbing Harris by the hair and slamming his face down into the center console.

"I've got the gun!" Max yelled.

Kris held Harris's head down while Max got out and climbed into the back seat, removing the second pistol from Harris's pocket. Then, using his own belt as well as Harris's he tied the man's hands and feet together.

"Good plan, partner," Max said, giving Kris a wide grin.

Taking the phone from her, Max reported in. Harris was lying sideways on the back seat floorboards, unable to do much more than moan at the moment.

After a hurried conversation in Navajo, Max closed up the phone. "They'll be here in ten minutes," he told Kris, then looked down at Harris. "Looks like your luck ran out, buddy."

It was more like five minutes when the big truck they'd seen earlier returned, followed closely by another, smaller pickup. Max pulled Harris out of the SUV and forced him down to his knees at gunpoint.

The man Max knew as Smoke came over to take charge of their prisoner, but as he drew near, Harris fell back and kicked out at him with both feet. Smoke sidestepped, grabbed Harris's feet, then flipped him over like a flapjack. Harris's face hit the ground with a crunch, and his body sagged.

"I didn't even see that coming," Kris whispered. "Your guy's fast."

"You should see him in a hand-to-hand," Max answered. "Harris won't be going anywhere except to jail."

A few moments later, Harris's bloodied face had been bandaged up and he was secured inside the cab of one of the trucks. Smoke came over then to meet them. "You'll have an escort now, so you can complete your mission without any more interruptions."

Max nodded once. "I had a vision and saw a certain place I'd like to check out. But my perspective in the vision was from above, as an eagle would see. To recognize that same place from ground level might take a little more time."

"No prob. Our people have your back—and yours," he added, looking at Kris. "*Hastiin Bigodii* thanks you for everything you've already done for our tribe, ma'am. But if you'd like, we can take you home now."

"Stay," Max said.

"Of course I'll stay. I need to see this through, too," she answered with a nod. "I always finish what I start."

A second man hurried up. "Leave the stargazer and his woman. We have to take the prisoner in now. There are people who want to talk to him before the police arrive."

Kris smiled as the men moved away. She was now the stargazer's woman. Somehow, she liked the sound of that.

IT WAS CLOSER TO DAWN than midnight when they reached the area Max had recognized. Kris had followed him in silence as they walked up the slope, headed for several trees at the top of a rocky knoll. The moon was shining brightly now and they'd been traveling in an almost straight line from the road. There was no need for a flashlight, although she had one in her hand, along with an empty canvas backpack for the platinum.

Although they weren't touching, instinct told her that Max could clearly sense her closeness. The connection between them was far more powerful than any she'd ever known. There was no doubt in her mind that they were meant for each other. Yet he'd still never spoken those three words her heart longed to hear. A simple "I love you" had no substitute.

"It's over this hilltop, several feet down the other side. Help me look for a stump about three feet high," he said, slowing down.

As they crossed the knoll, they found themselves on a moonlit slope where most of the trees had been harvested. Stumps, large and small, were everywhere.

"Which one?" she whispered.

Max gazed at the terrain. "I don't know, but it's here. We just need to find the right one."

Hearing a vehicle, they turned around quickly in a crouch. Max brought out Harris's pistol, motioning silently for Kris to stay low.

They heard running footsteps and, a minute later, Smoke came over the knoll. "I'm a friend," he called out, allowing the beam of his flashlight to bathe over him.

Max placed the pistol back into his belt as Smoke approached.

"Stargazer, I believe this belongs to you," Smoke said, holding out the missing *jish.* "One of our people found it in the arroyo by the winter camp. *Hastiin Bigodii* asked that it be returned to you immediately."

Max took it gratefully. The *jish* represented tradition, and the strength of the Navajo People. He was *Diné,* and by embracing the strength of his culture, he'd found himself.

Thanking his Navajo brother, he securely fastened the *jish* onto his belt. Then, trusting the vision, he made his way past the cluster of felled trees to one solitary stump on the next slope. When he looked down into it, he saw the fetish, and below that, the silver glint of platinum.

Max looked over at Kris as she handed him the backpack. "Our job's almost done. It's now time to return what was stolen from the tribe." Glancing at Smoke he added, "Stick around until I get this loaded, then follow us in."

THE CELEBRATION HELD at Window Rock a day later had been huge and continued throughout the night. The tribal president was in attendance as well as many others who, although they'd remained nameless to her, acknowledged her contribution to the case with respectful nods. One young boy had been given a special medicine bundle in exchange for the pocket knife he'd loaned Max.

Kris was watching a tribal musician playing the flute when Max came up behind her. Wrapping his arms around her waist, he pulled her into him. "We need to talk."

"Yes," she agreed eagerly. "But how?"

"Trust me." Taking her hand, he led her away from the crowd into an outcropping of statuesque piñons and scented junipers. Standing under the starlit sky, the waning moon visible above the deep red sandstone arch of Window Rock, he pressed the palm of her hand to his lips and held her gaze.

Everything inside her melted. How many women went through life never knowing what it was like to have the man they loved look at them like that? She could ask for nothing more.

"I've seen something. It was a vision that, at first, I couldn't completely understand because it wasn't like the others. Not static, but fluid—more like a beautiful possibility than a fact."

"What did you see?" she whispered, her heart racing.

"You pregnant with our child."

Kris smiled and pressed herself against him. "That's a beautiful possibility," she murmured into his neck.

"*Ayóó Ninshné*—I love you, Kris," he added, translating. "I can offer you a life filled with possibilities, but you came home looking for security and that's the one thing I can't give you. I'm a warrior, Kris. It's part of my nature," he said as the sound of drums rose from somewhere behind them.

"And part of the man I fell in love with," she answered softly.

"Will you be my wife?"

"Yes, Max Natoni," she said holding him tightly. "I'd like that very, very much."

THOROUGHBRED LEGACY
*The stakes are high when it comes to love,
horse racing, family secrets
and broken promises.*

*A new exciting Harlequin
continuity series coming soon!*
Led by New York Times *bestselling author
Elizabeth Bevarly*
FLIRTING WITH TROUBLE

Here's a preview!

THE DOOR CLOSED behind them, throwing them into darkness and leaving them utterly alone. And the next thing Daniel knew, he heard himself saying, "Marnie, I'm sorry about the way things turned out in Del Mar."

She said nothing at first, only strode across the room and stared out the window beside him. Although he couldn't see her well in the darkness—he still hadn't switched on a light…but then, neither had she—he imagined her expression was a little preoccupied, a little anxious, a little confused.

Finally, very softly, she said, "Are you?"

He nodded, then, worried she wouldn't be able to see the gesture, added, "Yeah. I am. I should have said goodbye to you."

"Yes, you should have."

Actually, he thought, there were a lot of things he should have done in Del Mar. He'd had *a lot* riding on the Pacific Classic, and even more on his entry, Little Joe, but after meeting Marnie, the Pacific Classic had been the last thing on Daniel's mind. His loss at Del Mar had pretty much ended his career before it had even begun, and he'd had to start all over again, rebuilding from nothing.

He simply had not then and did not now have room in his life for a woman as potent as Marnie Roberts. He was a horseman first and foremost. From the time he was a school-boy, he'd known what he wanted to do with his life—be the best possible trainer he could be.

He had to make sure Marnie understood—and he under-stood, too—why things had ended the way they had eight years ago. He just wished he could find the words to do that. Hell, he wished he could find the *thoughts* to do that.

"You made me forget things, Marnie, things that I really needed to remember. And that scared the hell out of me. Little Joe should have won the Classic. He was by far the best horse entered in that race. But I didn't give him the attention he needed and deserved that week, because all I could think about was you. Hell, when I woke up that morning all I wanted to do was lie there and look at you, and then wake you up and make love to you again. If I hadn't left when I did—the way I did—I might still be lying there in that bed with you, thinking about nothing else."

"And would that be so terrible?" she asked.

"Of course not," he told her. "But that wasn't why I was in Del Mar," he repeated. "I was in Del Mar to win a race. That was my job. And my work was the most important thing to me."

She said nothing for a moment, only studied his face in the darkness as if looking for the answer to a very important question. Finally she asked, "And what's the most important thing to you now, Daniel?"

Wasn't the answer to that obvious? "My work," he answered automatically.

She nodded slowly. "Of course," she said softly. "That is, after all, what you do best."

Her comment, too, puzzled him. She made it sound as if being good at what he did was a bad thing.

She bit her lip thoughtfully, her eyes fixed on his, glimmer-ing in the scant moonlight that was filtering through the window. And damned if Daniel didn't find himself wanting to pull her into his arms and kiss her. But as much as it might have felt as if no time had passed since Del Mar, there were eight years between now and then. And eight years was a long time in the best of circumstances. For Daniel and Marnie, it was virtually a lifetime.

So Daniel turned and started for the door, then halted. He couldn't just walk away and leave things as they were, unsettled. He'd done that eight years ago and regretted it.

"It *was* good to see you again, Marnie," he said softly. And since he was being honest, he added, "I hope we see each other again."

She didn't say anything in response, only stood silhouetted against the window with her arms wrapped around her in a way that made him wonder whether she was doing it because she was cold, or if she just needed something—someone—to hold on to. In either case, Daniel understood. There was an emptiness clinging to him that he suspected would be there for a long time.

* * * * *

THOROUGHBRED LEGACY
coming soon wherever books are sold!

Thoroughbred Legacy

Launching in June 2008

A dramatic new 12-book continuity that embodies the American Dream.

Meet the Prestons, owners of Quest Stables, a successful horse-racing and breeding empire. But the lives, loves and reputations of this hardworking family are put at risk when a breeding scandal unfolds.

Flirting with Trouble

by *New York Times* bestselling author

ELIZABETH BEVARLY

Eight years ago, publicist Marnie Roberts spent seven days of bliss with Australian horse trainer Daniel Whittleson. But just as quickly, he disappeared. Now Marnie is heading to Australia to finally confront the man she's never been able to forget.

The stakes are high when it comes to love, horse racing, family secrets and broken promises.

A new exciting Harlequin continuity series coming soon!

www.eHarlequin.com

REQUEST YOUR FREE BOOKS!

2 FREE NOVELS
PLUS 2
FREE GIFTS!

Breathtaking Romantic Suspense

HI08

Cole's Red-Hot Pursuit

Cole Westmoreland is a man who gets what he wants. And he wants independent and sultry Patrina Forman! She resists him—until a Montana blizzard traps them together. For three delicious nights, Cole indulges Patrina with his brand of seduction. When the sun comes out, Cole and Patrina are left to wonder—will this be the end of the passion that storms between them?

Look for

COLE'S RED-HOT PURSUIT

by USA TODAY bestselling author

BRENDA JACKSON

Available in June 2008 wherever you buy books.

Always Powerful, Passionate and Provocative.

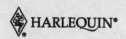

HARLEQUIN®

INTRIGUE®

COMING NEXT MONTH

#1065 LOADED by Joanna Wayne
Four Brothers of Colts Run Cross
Oil impresario Matt Collingsworth couldn't abide his name being dragged through the mud. So when Shelly Lane insisted his family's huge Texas spread held devastating secrets, Matt was a gentleman all the way—and saved her from certain death.

#1066 UNDERCOVER COMMITMENT by Kathleen Long
The Body Hunters
Eileen Caldwell never imagined she'd walk into her past and find Kyle Landenburg waiting for her. The Body Hunter had saved her life once before—would history repeat?

#1067 STRANGERS IN THE NIGHT by Kerry Connor
Thriller
Bounty hunter Gideon Ross thought he could protect Allie Freeman, but he didn't even know her. In a game of survival, whoever keeps their secret the longest wins.

#1068 WITH THE M.D....AT THE ALTAR? by Jessica Andersen
The Curse of Raven's Cliff
When the town was hit with a mysterious epidemic, was Roxanne Peterson's only shot at survival a forced marriage to Dr. Luke Freeman?

#1069 THE HEART OF BRODY McQUADE by Mallory Kane
The Silver Star of Texas: Cantera Hills Investigation
People said the only thing Brody McQuade kept close to his heart was his gun. Was prominent attorney Victoria Kirkland the only one brave enough to poke holes in his defense?

#1070 PROTECTIVE INSTINCTS by Julie Miller
The Precinct: Brotherhood of the Badge
Detective Sawyer Kincaid had the best instincts in the department. And only by standing between Melissa Teague and danger could he keep this single mother safe from harm.

www.eHarlequin.com

HICNM0508R